for Livi and Abby
sqn

NICKING TIME

T.TRAYNOR

Kelpies is an imprint of Floris Books
First published in 2013 by Floris Books
© 2013 T. Traynor

T. Traynor has asserted her right under the
Copyright, Designs and Patent Act 1988 to be
identified as the Author of this work

The publisher acknowledges subsidy from
Creative Scotland towards the publication of this volume

 This book is also available
as an eBook

British Library CIP data available
ISBN 978-086315-955-8

Printed in Poland

References to IRN-BRU® and "Made in Scotland From Girders"
are used with kind permission of A.G. BARR plc

1

"This one's for Midge," says Bru. "The ship's going down and you can only save one person. What'd you choose: to save Skooshie or to save Hector?"

"I can't answer that!" I protest. Skooshie and Hector look at me, interested, waiting.

We're in the den: Bru, Skooshie, Hector, Lemur and me. It's the night before the last day of school. Tomorrow – at long last – the summer holidays start. So we're playing a celebratory round of Skooshie's Game. Well, I say "Skooshie's Game". Skooshie didn't really invent it, not as a game. He just kept asking questions that gave us a choice: "What'd you choose: to eat a raw egg or eat a raw sausage? What'd you choose: to play football for England or never play football again? What'd you choose: to be an ancient Roman or a Martian?" He was just genuinely interested in knowing. We got tired of always answering, so we made it into a game. This way we get the chance to think up some questions too. It's called Skooshie's Game in his honour.

"You've got to answer," says Bru. "That's the rules."

"It is the rules, Midge," Skooshie agrees, like I don't know that.

"Let's think," I say. "Well. Hector did promise me a loan of those old Victor comics over the holidays, so I'm thinking maybe him." (Bellow of protest from Skooshie.) "But – but – I hadn't finished – if he *did* go down with the ship, his mum knows what a big Victor fan I am, so she might *give* me the comics to keep. Ow!" (Unidentified missile hits me in the head, coming from Hector's direction.) "It's tricky."

"We need an answer," says Lemur.

"Obviously I'd save Skooshie, because Hector's got his 5,000 metres badge – he's going to get to the shore on his own no problem. So I can concentrate on helping Skoosh."

"Nice one," says Hector, and Skooshie grins his approval too.

"What if neither of them could swim?" asks Bru.

"Well, (1) they can, and (2) you're not allowed to change the question after I've answered it."

"Fair enough." Bru prods the white paper bag with his foot hopefully. But it's empty, as he suspected, the white chocolate mice, flying saucers and strawberry laces long gone. He settles back on the big settee cushions waiting for me to ask a question. The cushions are one of the big improvements that we've made to the den in the past few weeks. We dragged them out of a skip in Stanmore Road.

We've spent a lot of time getting the den perfect for this summer. We used it a bit last year. But it was freezing cold in the winter. And there was the risk we'd be discovered, once the trees lost their leaves, so we didn't go there that much. Now we've managed to make it more or less waterproof. We're careful about how often we go in and out, and we never do it all at the same time – we don't want to attract any attention. It's taken a while to perfect our techniques. Now we're like spies losing a tail – I think MI6 would be lucky to have us. Or at the very least we should be in the next Bond film.

The brilliant thing about our den is how hidden it is. There are gardens on both sides, and at the other end of the gardens, houses. On the right – that's the right if you're sitting on the cushions, facing the entrance – on the right, tenements running up Stanmore Road (where Hector lives); on the left, the big expensive houses on May Terrace. At the end of both of the gardens are huge big trees and thick bushes. The Stanmore Road people think their garden backs onto the May Terrace gardens. The May Terrace people think the same. But they don't. There's a space in between. And that's where our den is.

No one knows it's there. No one knows how to get into it except us.

"OK. Hector, what'd you choose," I say. "A pet chihuahua or a pet piranha?"

"Too easy," says Hector. "Piranha, obviously. Who wouldn't want a man-eating fish as a pet?"

"Yes, but a chihuahua – a dog you can keep in your pocket? You could take it to school with you. Magic!"

"You would have to *remember* that you had it in your pocket," says Skooshie. "What if you forget and you're playing football and you're in goal and you dive to save a shot and – **SPLAT**!!!"

He follows this up with an impression of a splatted chihuahua that has us howling with laughter and rolling on the ground. He's really talented, Skooshie.

Next Hector comes up with a question for Lemur. "What'd you choose: never be able to talk again or have hair like a girl?" We like the inventiveness of this one, and the fact it's so brilliantly meant for Lemur. If we ever had a competition to see who could manage to stay silent for longest (and we should some time – it would be interesting), Lemur would be first one out. Within a minute, guaranteed. He really cannot shut up.

He's torn.

"Would I have to *wear* it like a girl?" he asks. "I mean, if it's long, would I have to wear it in those bunch things they have on the sides of their heads? Or could I just have it long and messy, you know, like a pirate or a wild man?"

"Oh, I never thought of that," says Hector. "Glad you asked. I'm thinking *definitely* bunches."

"And ribbons," chips in Skooshie.

Lemur looks like he's in pain.

"Pink ribbons," says Bru.

"Or never talk, ever again," I add helpfully. "Not a word."

There's a mumble from Lemur.

"I beg your pardon?" says Hector, leaning towards him. "I don't think we heard that."

"Girl's hair!" Lemur roars.

As we whoop and laugh, Skooshie tries to grab a bunchful of Lemur's hair to see what he'd look like. The game's a bogey until Lemur manages to fight him off.

"I've got one for all of you," says Lemur. "What'd you choose: family or friends?"

"Friends," says Skooshie firmly.

"Friends," echoes Hector.

"Friends." Bru thrusts his arm out and one by one we slap our hands on top of his.

"Friends," I say. And as mine is the hand on top, I start us off on a chorus of *The Flashing Blade* theme tune. It feels like a good way to almost kick off the holidays.

When we can hardly see each other inside the den, we have to give in to the fact that it's time to go home. It doesn't feel as bad as it might because we know that from tomorrow we'll have time to do whatever we want. Hector reminds us to get here as soon as possible after school.

"We've a lot to plan," he says. "Cathkin," he adds meaningfully.

"Definitely," says Lemur. "Definitely Cathkin this holiday."

We separate on Prospecthill Road: Hector and Skooshie to head down Bolivar Terrace, Lemur to double back along May Terrace, and Bru and me to cross the road to the flats.

"See youse later," says Skooshie as he leaves us.

"*Youse?* What do you mean, *youse?* There's no such word," says Lemur. Lemur likes to be right.

"Well, there is, actually," says Hector. Hector likes to be right too. "If you're talking about a lot of female sheep..."

"Is that what you're saying, Skoosh? You're telling us about your plans to watch farm animals? *Baaaaa!* "

"It's a thingummy," says Skooshie, aiming a good-natured kick in Lemur's direction. "A... plural. *You* for one person, *youse* for more than one. Otherwise it would be confusing. I mean, if I say, '*You*'re an eejit', I want *youse* all to know I mean *you*, Lemur, not all of *youse* at once."

He's got a point.

"I'm really looking forward to the holidays," says Bru, as we walk slowly down the hill.

"Me too."

We don't talk about why. We know it's more than just an ordinary summer and that we're expecting great things to happen. It has to be the best summer we've ever had because we're all scared it's going to be the last one. That at the end of it secondary school will swallow us up and make us different and everything might change between us.

But secondary's miles off. The summer stretches ahead as far as we can see, six totally endless sunny weeks.

2

"Are you planning to leave that there?"

My mum points at my uniform, in a pile on the floor, with an accusing finger.

"But I won't need it again."

"So we can just step over it every day for the next six years, until you drop the next one on top of it? Pick it up!"

Can she not see that I'm in a hurry? I think about mentioning this but she has a habit of making this kind of discussion go on and on. Quicker just to do it. I bundle the clothes into the dirty-washing basket. My tie sneaks out again, like an escaping striped snake.

"Be back at 5 for dinner!"

"I will!" I pull the door shut behind me. I run down the stairs, all twelve flights, because it will take too long to wait for the lift. It does mean I have less puff to get up the hill – I manage to make it to the end of the fencing round the car park. Not bad. My aim is to make it all the way to the top without stopping. I reckon I'll be able to do it by the end of the holidays.

They're already waiting for me in the den. When I come in, they give me a "Hey" and a wave and continue what sounds like quite a time-consuming conversation about how little time we've got to do everything. Hector has a scrap of paper in front of him and a well-chewed pencil in his hand.

"We've got a lot to fit in," Bru's saying.

"Time is always against us," Hector adds.

"Yeah," says Skooshie. "It's always either going too quickly or much much too slowly, don't you find?"

"Wouldn't it be great," says Lemur, "if you could bank time?"

"What d'you mean?"

"If you could save time that wasn't wanted, then use it when it was."

"I get it," says Bru.

"I don't," says Skooshie.

"Well, let's say your mum makes you go to the shops with her on a day when she's buying *everything* and it takes forever," says Bru. "That's an hour you're never going to get back. But say you could. Say you could take that hour – move straight from the first shop to the minute when she's putting everything away in the kitchen cupboard and giving you a biscuit for being helpful. You could take that hour and stash it for a time when you want to use it. For example, if we were playing a really exciting game of rounders and it was getting dark and we all had to go home. But, oh ho, here's that spare hour I squirrelled away earlier. I've been keeping it just for this very thing – I'll use it now, so let's finish the game."

We're impressed. We like this idea.

"So it's like a time piggy bank," I say.

"Yeah – but not one of those annoying ones you have to break to get at the money."

"So you actually get the time for playing rounders *and* the biscuit for helping with the shopping?" Hector looks doubtful. He's got a point.

"Yeah," says Skooshie. "That's not likely, is it?"

"What if you *didn't* get the biscuit but you *didn't* get told off for not helping?" I suggest.

"Your mum just... forgot?" says Lemur.

"Yeah."

We're happy with this as a compromise.

"So, do we put 'Invent Time Bank' on the list of things we want to do this summer?" asks Skooshie.

"Might as well," I say.

"OK," says Hector, scribbling. "That's number 7."

"Read them out, Hector," says Lemur.

"In no particular order – apart from the first one:

1. Cathkin. "

"Even if we do *nothing* else," says Skooshie, "we do that. I would underline it, Hector, just so that's clear."

As if we're going to forget that one. This has been our ambition forever, to get into Cathkin. Cathkin's the derelict football park that is right next to the flats – I mean, *right next to* them. It was abandoned before the flats were built – otherwise we could've seen all the games for free from my living-room window. You might have heard of it – it used to be the old Hampden Park, before they built the huge one. Scotland even played England there once: that's how brilliant it is. (1–nil to us – **YAAAAAAAARGH!**) Anyway, now Cathkin's all boarded up: big, corrugated metal sheets nailed across the entrances, mesh fences running right round the park, the works. As if that wasn't enough, we're also completely and totally forbidden to go in there. To us it looks like a giant Christmas present, tied up with barbed wire: our name's on the gift tag, but it's just never stopped being November... Until now. Now we've decided it's Christmas Eve. Now it's time. This holiday we're going in.

Hector continues his reading of The List.

"2. Football

3. Tennis

4. Queen's Park

5. Scavy hunt

6. Games/Competitions."

"Are you not listing the games, Hector?"

"Too many. You know the kind of thing: Hospital Tig, hill-rolling, Kick the Can, water fight, etc, etc, etc."

"Sounds good."

"And 7. Invent Time Bank. Have we forgotten anything?"

Head shakes all round.

"Wait a minute," says Hector, scanning the list. "This is all sunny-weather stuff. What if it rains?"

"If it rains we'll have plenty of time to make another list."

"Anyway, it's not going to rain."

"So, when are we going to Cathkin?"

"Tomorrow! Tomorrow!"

"It's more complicated than that. It all depends on Midge's mum."

"Is she coming as well?"

"Oh, ha ha, Bru. No, we need to do it at a time when there's no chance she'll see us."

"Which is when?"

"Well," says Hector, who's been thinking strategically. "It'll have to be an evening, because the sun will be shining directly on Midge's side of the flats at that time of day."

"So?"

"So everybody will have their blinds drawn!" Hector's particularly pleased with this bit of reasoning – he worked it out the other week. "That means there's much less chance of being spotted by neighbours who'll tell Midge's mum what we've been up to."

"OK, so an evening."

"Then we have to bear in mind Midge's dad."

I'm suddenly the focus of attention, and not in a good way. Everybody except Hector is looking at me. I can tell they're wondering if we're going to be working through my entire family, each person presenting a different and annoying problem.

"Do he and your mum take turns looking out the window?"

"No. My dad's on night shift. So he comes out the flats just before it gets dark. He always looks for me to make sure I'm OK and tells me to go up in ten minutes. If we're not around for that, it's going to raise suspicions."

"So the plan is that we're going to Cathkin on the 24th of don't-hold-your-breath?"

"No, no, it's happening. As luck would have it, Midge's mum goes out on one of the evenings Midge's dad is off work – Fridays!"

"So, tomorrow? Aw, yeah!"

"Ah... we can't go tomorrow. Or at least I can't."

"Why not?" We're all looking at Bru now, which is nicer for me but not so good for him.

"The Whistle-Blower thing. I'm kept in. D'you not remember?"

We groan. We remember, all too well.

"I'm lucky I got out today, to be honest," says Bru. "Sorry."

"We need to get her back!" says Lemur. Because although Bru was the victim, nobody is more intent on getting revenge against Mrs Whistle-Blower than Lemur.

I'd better fill you in on the whole story.

Mrs Whistle-Blower lives in the third block of flats – the one that's not mine and not Bru's. There are no kids in that block, not one. It's all old folk: I mean, imagine...

Mrs Whistle-Blower's not her actual name (there aren't a lot of double-barrelled people round our flats) – we call her that because of her favourite hobby. She likes to lie in wait for us to go and play tennis down by the lock-ups. At the first sound of a ball bounce, she leans out her window and tells us to get lost. And she blows her whistle to emphasise her point. Or possibly she's hoping to stir up reinforcements, other old people who'll lean out their windows and shout at us. What would you rather hear in the background while you're watching television: the happy plink-plonk of kids playing tennis? Or an ear-splitting whistle and shrill complaining? She's a menace.

So one day Bru's out without us, looking after his wee brothers, Kenny and Graham (also known as the Toaty Terrors). They're playing Hide and Seek, and before Bru knows it, Kenny's run into Mrs Whistle-Blower's flats. So he shoots in after him to try and flush him out. Kenny knows he shouldn't be in there, which makes the chase that much more fun for him. He starts circling the lift, running round and round the ground floor, shrieking like a girl, with Bru in pursuit, trying desperately to shush him. Then Mrs WB comes stomping down. (Not sure if she had her whistle on her – it might have burst all their eardrums if she'd blown it in that confined space.)

Next thing she's telling on Bru to his mum. Says Bru wasn't looking after Kenny and Graham properly *and* that he was really cheeky when she told him off. *Bru* says he said (to Kenny), "Stop being a brat!" *She* says Bru said, "You're annoying the old bat." (See? All that whistling – really bad for your hearing.) She gets Bru into a lot of trouble. A LOT. He's got to go up to her door and apologise – for something he hasn't even done! We all offered to go with him (Kenny wouldn't go – and he wasn't made to – wee toe rag!), but Bru's mum wouldn't let us. She said Mrs WB'd had enough noise and disruption without us all turning up on her doorstep. As if *that* wasn't bad enough, Bru's also grounded for the first three days of the holiday. No Cathkin this Friday.

"Spiteful old witch," says Lemur, in full flow now. "Really – we can't let her get away with this." His eyes are glinting at the thought of who-knows-what wild idea. He takes anything that hurts his friends very seriously, Lemur.

"We'd be caught," says Hector sadly. "We'd be in big trouble – big kept-in kind of trouble – more than three days. And then where would we be?"

He's right. It's not worth the risk. Even Lemur seems to accept that. For now.

"Our time will come," he says.

"So that's a whole nother week we'll need to wait for Cathkin!" Skooshie's getting so disheartened he's starting to inflict violence on words.

Everybody feels fed up or discouraged sometimes. Even Bru, who you can rely on to cheer you up in almost any situation. But not Lemur. Lemur's never low, not ever. When I think of Lemur, d'you know what I hear in my head? Him saying: "C'MON!" It's his battle cry. It's hard to resist.

"*C'mon!* We're nearly there. It'll give us time to get a brilliant plan together. *Next* Friday we'll be standing on the pitch! Trust me. Are we on?"

"We're on!"

3

"What's for dinner? It's not that yellow fish, is it? The disgusting salty one that tastes like evil?"

"I feel sorry for him," says my mum. "Ham and macaroni. He doesn't seem to have anybody – you don't see any family coming to visit. It's terrible to be that lonely when you're old."

"Who are you talking about?"

"A new neighbour – Mr Murphy. He's got the Browns' old house. And that yellow fish, for your information, is very expensive."

"Another old guy, Dad."

"I know. Glasgow Corporation definitely has a factory that makes them and sends them here."

"Yes – he's not long moved in. And he's on his own. You nip up to see him on your way out after dinner, James, and ask if there's anything he needs."

"Aw, Mum – not tonight! It's the start of the holidays. I'm only back for dinner."

"Tomorrow then. In the morning."

"OK, in the morning I will."

"So, the holidays at last. D'you have lots of plans

with Bru and that lot?" asks my dad when we sit down to eat.

I nod, my mouth full of macaroni.

"What plans?" asks Kit. She's my sister. She's really nosy.

"Stuff," I answer, scooping in another mouthful.

"That's the door," says my mum. "How quickly do your friends eat?"

It turns out not to be Bru as expected, but Skooshie. He's still eating, in fact. The remains of a giant sausage roll in a City Bakeries bag.

"Hullo, Mrs Laird. Hullo, Mr Laird."

"Sit down in the living room, Mark. James isn't finished yet."

Instead Skooshie leans in the kitchen doorway, up for a chat while we eat.

"D'you want a drink, Skooshie?" I ask.

"No, thanks. I've got one here." He produces a can of Irn-Bru.

"Skooshie – how d'you get that name?" asks my dad.

"Well, from McCuish. Mark McCuish – Cush – Skoosh – Skooshie."

"Aw, right," says my dad. "So what about Bru? Where's that from?"

Kit and I look at each other, like he's daft.

"Because he's ginger," we say at the same time.

"Aw, I get it... And Hector is..."

"And Hector's called Hector because there are three Alans in our class," says Skooshie. "It would be confusing to call them all Alan," he adds helpfully.

"Right..."

"And James is Midge because it's Jim backwards, I'm guessing."

Kit chips in, "No, it's Midge short for Midgie – because he's small, noisy and annoying."

"Yeah and I bite!" I lunge at her and she squeals.

"Behave, you two," says my mum. "Lemur's the one that's always confused me. Why d'you call him that?"

"From the polis alphabet," says Skooshie, trying not to rift. The ginger bubbles force their way out of his nose instead, noisily. My mum gives him a Look.

"Eh?" says my dad. The whole ginger-nose-bubbles thing has made Skooshie's last comment a bit hard to follow.

"You know, Mr Laird. When they have words for the letters, so the polis don't get the wrong spelling? So, his initials are CL – in polis talk that's Charlie Lemur."

"Is that right?" My dad takes a swig of his tea and looks amused.

I roll my eyes. "What can you do, Dad? We've given up telling Skoosh it's *Lima*. Lemur's just stuck."

"Lemur suits him," says Skooshie. "They're wee monkeys, aren't they? Always jumping about the place."

"So you'd be Juliet?" says Kit, grinning like the evil panda she is.

"Shut up, Cursed-y. That's Bru at the door, Mum. Can I go?"

"Yes. Take some biscuits for pudding. Be back before it's dark. What are you all up to tomorrow?"

"Dunno yet. Bru's ... eh, he's not ... around for a few days. Monday we're all playing football at the recs," I say, getting out the biscuit tin and prising the lid off.

"Big game," says Skooshie.

I'm presuming she meant biscuits for everyone? I don't want to be rude just sitting eating on my own. I cram five mint Viscounts in my pocket. The biscuit tin's looking a bit empty after that, so I space out the ones that are left with my finger, then jam on the lid hard and put it back in the cupboard. My mum raises her eyebrows, then decides to be pleased I've tidied up and gives me a smile.

"Thanks, Mum. See you all later."

"Midge, can we play Go when you get back?" Kit yells.

"OK," I yell back.

"Is that the game where you travel round the world collecting souvenirs?" says Bru. "The one we played at Christmas?"

"Yeah." We're going down in the lift because we're all still a bit full. "Kit and I played it every single day in the Christmas holidays, if not with you then with my mum and dad. Then it disappeared. But Kit found it again on top of the wardrobe the other day and we're back into it."

"It's funny how toys do disappear like that sometimes," says Bru. "Or break really unexpectedly. It happened with my brothers' guns – remember those ones that lit up and went **WA-WA-WA-WA-WA**? One day – fine; next day – no lights, no noise, nothing. My mum said it was because they'd used them too much and maybe next time they'd learn. I said it might just be the batteries but she said it definitely wasn't, she'd checked and so had Dad, and it definitely was just one of those things, what a shame."

"Why *is* Hector called Hector?" Skooshie asks, as we walk up the hill.

"After the soldier in the Trojan War," says Bru. "D'you not remember Mr McKie telling us the stories in Primary 5?"

"Did the Trojans not lose the war?"

"Yeah, they did," I say. "But only because the Greeks were dirty cheats. That whole horse thing."

"Oh, yeah. I remember our Hector always wanting to play the other Hector when we had the battles," says Skooshie.

"Yeah." We don't say anything for a minute, remembering. Our class had been the Trojans and 5B had been the Greeks. We'd rewritten history on more than one occasion.

"They were good, those fights," says Skooshie.

"Yeah," Bru agrees. "And so after that Hector was Hector for evermore."

"And what's Lemur's real name?" asks Skooshie.

We think hard.

"Charlie," I say. "I think it might actually be Charlie."

"I thought it was Callum," says Bru, shrugging.

"Maybe it's one of those names that are really a surname," says Skooshie. "You know, like Crawford or Cameron or Colquhoun. He's posh enough."

"Colquhoun?" Bru snorts. "D'you not think if his name was Colquhoun, we'd've come up with a better nickname than Lemur?"

"Colquhoun," says Skooshie with his thinking face on. "Colquhoun, Colquhoun, your neighbourhood loon."

"I never saw him as a Colquhoun," I say. "We'll have to ask him."

"It must be bad, whatever is it," says Bru with a grin, "if he's kept it that quiet."

By the time we get to the den, we've forgotten. Hector and Lemur are arguing about the best way to get into Cathkin and they're in dire need of our opinions. There's just too much on our minds to be bothering about trivial things. We do find out later though. It turns out not to be Colquhoun, in case you're wondering.

4

With the constant talking about Cathkin, we're really in the mood for a proper game of football. We can't do much about that till we get Bru back. We spend most of the next three days cursing Mrs Whistle-Blower and her evil influence and moaning about the unfairness of Bru being kept in. We take turns saying, "I mean, *right at the start of the holidays!*" and "I know – unbelievable!" Luckily we've got Monday to look forward to.

There's nowhere to play football round the flats – there's plenty of grass, but it's all hilly. When I look out the living-room window at the perfect green of the Cathkin pitch, I think, "So near and yet so far." Ironic, eh? (I used this as an example of irony in my entrance exam: As I am a football fan, it is ironic that I live within spitting distance of a former professional football pitch that nobody wants to use and where I am not allowed to play. I didn't say "spitting distance" – I said something like "right next to". But I reckon I *could* spit the distance. If you took the window-locks off so I could get some momentum.)

To get a proper game, we have to go to the recs. They're between us and Queen's Park: six grit football pitches surrounded by loads of grass. You have to time it right – Sunday afternoons are hopeless, with all the local amateur teams out playing in their competitive leagues. During the holidays, when they're all at work, you've more chance. Monday morning we reclaim Bru and set off, armed with a ball and some bottles of water so we don't collapse in the heat.

It's a fair way but we don't mind the walk. It's become more interesting recently, since we did Mary, Queen of Scots at school. Before then I hadn't really wondered why the area by the recs is called Battlefield. We were amazed to find out something interesting had actually happened around here.

"So this is the route Mary's army would have followed on the way to the battle," says Hector, inspiring us to set up a forced march. Our stomping feet hit the pavement in rhythm, *left, two, three, four, left, two, three, four* in honour of the soldiers that hoofed it up Prospecthill Road and down the other side four hundred years ago.

"Ooof!" says Bru, when the marching comes to a ragged stop after a short distance. "I wouldn't fancy doing that in armour!"

He then nudges me sideways, and punches me hard in the arm. "Free Punch!" he shouts.

I'm annoyed I've been caught. The metal covering in the pavement is small but the letters **FP** are clear enough and should have been really obvious to me. He nudged me to make me stand on it, which is fair. And when I stood on it, he had the right to punch me. I can't punch him back. That's the rule with fire hydrants: you stand on one that says **FP**, somebody's allowed to give you a free punch; if it says **FH**, they get a free hit, which is the more fun one of the two because it gives you a bit more scope.

"Which one's your house, Lemur?" Hector asks.

Lemur waves vaguely in the direction of May Terrace, a small road set back from the main road and shielded from it by a row of trees. It's hard to see which one he means. The houses in May Terrace are big and the people living there have expensive cars. "They're a bit pan loaf for us," my dad says. He had to explain that one for Kit. "We're plain loaf kind of people – rougher made and with harder crusts."

"I'd invite you all in," says Lemur. "But my parents aren't there and I don't have a key." We've never been to Lemur's house. It's true we're a generally mucky group, and a bit clumsy. Maybe his mum's worried we'll make a mess. Come to think of it, I've never been to Skooshie's either. It's not really on our way anywhere and Skooshie's always the first to suggest hanging out at our houses.

"Did you know," says Hector, "that after the Battle of Langside, the dead soldiers were buried in nearby marshland? Marshland that would later become the Queen's Park boating pond..."

"Whoah! We need to go back there soon!"

"Do you think if you leaned over the edge of the boat and looked into the water you might see them, looking up at you?"

"Or find some of their swords at the bottom of the pond?"

This gem of information is definitely one of Hector's finest offerings. He walks the rest of the way smiling, quietly pleased with the effect it's had.

"I reckon it's the pitch right at the end on the left. Just before the pedestrian crossing to the park," says Bru.

Every time we come here we debate this. It is important because it affects where we play, presuming we have a choice of pitches. Today we do.

"D'you not think," says Hector, like this is the first time he's really thought about it, "that it's more over to the right? I think that's more likely."

"Based on what, Hector?" I ask, because somebody has to.

"Well." He puts his hand to his forehead and scans the land. He's either doing it to keep the sun out of his eyes or he's trying to get into the role of army commander. "It just feels like it would be more over to the right. Douglas of Drumlanrig's cavalry sweeps down from the hill there." (This accompanied by big sweeping gesture.) "Herries's cavalry advances to stop him there." (This accompanied by big stopping gesture.) "Yeah. I think they would've clashed right by that goal post."

To be honest, there must've been horses all over the place in the Battle of Langside. I'm not convinced it comes down to one pitch or another. But I've tried this argument before and nobody listens.

"We played on that one last time," says Bru. It's his

football, which kind of means he has dibs on choosing. But he never picks fights, Bru. He just bides his time, not backing down.

"Yeah, we did," says Hector at last, and he starts to walk towards Bru's pitch.

I'll pass over the bit where they debate who should play in what direction because it's just more of the same. This on top of the fact that five's an awkward number for football, so we've got plenty to discuss and decide without bringing in historical factors. We're still debating who's on which side and whether somebody should be a referee or whether we should take turns being goalie and do four-on-one striking practice when we're interrupted.

"Hey. D'you want a game?"

It's a gang of lads, six of them, about our age. (What would be a good collective noun for that, I wonder? My teacher said collective nouns would be big in the grammar exam, so I had to learn a lot of them. Maybe *a litter of lads. A boisterousness of boys. A squabble of squirts. A posse of pals.* I file them away, meaning to tell them to Kit later and see what she thinks.)

"Yes," says Lemur. "Us against you?"

"You're on."

I got it wrong. The phrase I was looking for was *a batallion of boys.* Because when we start playing it's very clear that this is a battle. And it doesn't look like we're on the side that's going to win.

Because it hasn't rained for a long time, the pitches are dry and throw up clouds of orange dust when you run, when you pass, when you fall. And we fall often. They're determined to win and they don't care how. They tackle hard. I feel like a soldier in the thick of things. Sometimes I think I may have mislaid my sword and shield. We do fight back but, in what seems like no time at all, they've managed to slip the ball not once but twice past our defences and into the goal.

"HALF-TIME!" yells Lemur. We stop running about and collapse on the grass at the side of the pitch, a strategic distance from the other team. All you can hear for a minute is the sound of eleven boys panting and the glurping of water. Then Lemur calls us to attention.

"We haven't been playing as a team," he says in a hushed voice that won't reach the enemy. "But we're only 2–nil down. We can turn this around. Bru, you go wider on the left – they look a bit weak there. Skooshie, you go forward with Bru and get the ball to him whenever you can. Midge, focus on blocking the big lad who scored the two goals – pass it forward when you get the chance, but stay back. Don't go forward yourself – it makes us too vulnerable at the back. Hector – the goals weren't your fault – we all slipped up. I'll be right in front of you. Tell me where you need me to move to help stop them scoring. OK? Everybody keep talking to each other so we know what we're doing. *C'MON!*"

We don't question any of it. To be honest, he's not that great a player, Lemur, but as a captain we trust him.

"Let's give it laldy, lads," says Skooshie as a final morale-booster and we trot back onto the pitch.

This half starts with a skirmish in the centre, which ends with Skooshie sitting on his bum in the dust. He looks like he's going to punch somebody but Lemur runs over and pulls him up, shouting, "*C'mon,* let's play!" Skooshie wipes his hands on his shorts and scowls with determination. The next minute he's got the ball. Bru's calling for it. Skooshie passes wide, a confident, clean shot that finds its target. Bru's round the last defender and the ball's in the net. Yes!

We restart.

They're down in our half now. I manage to intercept a pass and get the ball out to Bru, but he's tackled and loses it. The ball comes back, over my head, falling between Lemur and a ginger kid on the other team. They both go for it, colliding and sprawling on the ground. Even as they're falling, Lemur's shouting to me. I dive back, retrieving the ball. I look up. Bru's covered but Skooshie's in a space and he's waving wildly – he wants me to pass to him. I dummy to the left but chip the ball straight to Skooshie. He charges forward, flips the ball sideways onto his right foot and shoots. GOAL!

The other team is looking tired. We're tired too – but we're also feeling like we could do anything. We pause for an unofficial break, taking swigs of water. By now it's really really hot.

"The next goal wins it?" says the captain of the other team.

"Agreed," says Lemur.

They come at us with the force of cannon fire. I don't know where they've got the energy from. Maybe it's the thought that this is it, if they can just score once more, it will be over. We're pushed right back into our half, but Lemur waves Bru and Skooshie away. We – me, Lemur, Hector – need to stop them and give Bru and Skooshie the chance to win the game for us. The ball powers through, just beyond my reach. Lemur lunges at it but misses it too. It's all on Hector – he dives, arms outstretched, hitting the ground hard. When the dust clears we can see him hugging the ball tightly to his chest, his grin the only white thing in his orange face.

"HEC–TOR! HEC–TOR! HEC–TOR!" Skoo-shie's chanting, punching the air with relief.

From Hector to Lemur. A neat pass to me. I take it forward – it looks like there's space for me to go by myself. But I see Skooshie tying up the attention of two of the other team as he darts about and Bru unmarked. I punt the ball up the field in Bru's direction. He collects it on the run. He's got their attention now, but it's too late. He's running fast into the gap, the ball at his feet – and then it's shooting into the net. 3–2!!!

"Thanks for the game." The losers limp off, the forces of evil defeated.

We're stained orange-red with the efforts of battle: our shoes, shorts, t-shirts, knees, elbows. Lemur's hair even looks bloodied with it. We are ecstatic. We've enough money between us for celebratory ice cream from the Mount Florida Café on the way home.

We walk back up Prospecthill Road, groaning at its steepness, and, licking our ice creams, we re-live the highlights of the match.

5

Today's Wednesday – two days to Cathkin! – so for once I'm not out early. Wednesday's the day *The Flashing Blade* is on in the morning. Kit and I are still in our pyjamas, waiting for it to start. To create a cinema effect, we've closed the curtains and the door to the kitchen, so the television is the only bright thing in the room. We're lying on the floor on top of all the cushions from the settee, which we've piled up just in front of the screen. Everybody knows not to disturb us during *The Flashing Blade*, so when the door goes, we ignore it. It won't be for us. Anybody we'd want to see is at this moment in their own house, glued to their own telly.

"It's Lemur," says my mum, showing him in.

He's out of breath from running.

"Can I watch?" he asks, collapsing onto the cushions beside me. He has just made it before the music starts, lucky for him. Kit and I sing along, as usual. *You've got to fight for what you want, For all that you believe!* The beat of the music fits the mad galloping of the horses as the fighters ride across endless fields, determined to save France. We're word perfect. We've practised – a lot. Lemur does not know the words. Lemur has never seen *The Flashing Blade.* I don't know how this is even possible. It is *probably* the best series in the history of television. I say *probably* because *Dr Who* is a contender, of course. (Must remember to use that one in the next Skooshie's Game: *The Flashing Blade* or *Dr Who*? How will Lemur begin to answer that one, with these sorts of gaps in his knowledge? Sometimes you've got to wonder whether he's quite as clever as he seems.) To go back to the whole *Flashing Blade/Dr Who* debate, maybe it comes down to this: if you were to ask me, Midge Laird, age twelve, of Glasgow, Scotland, if I'd rather be François, the Chevalier de Recci, or a time lord, I'd say, "Pass me my sword!"

"What they're saying doesn't fit what their mouths are doing," Lemur points out.

"Shut up," I warn him. "Watch now, talk later."

It's the opening episode. The castle is under attack from the Spanish, who think they're going to storm it easy-peasy. They hit it with one cannonball after another. It's already a smoking ruin and you can't see how the people inside the castle can possibly hold out. But this is the one where the French heroes, François and Guillot, sneak up behind the Spanish troops and start firing on them with their own spare cannons. They set fire to a barrel of gunpowder in a horse-drawn cart and send the horses careering madly into the Spanish camp. It's infectious, the obvious delight of François and Guillot. They laugh like madmen – big **HA HA HA HA!** laughs – and jump up and down with joy as the

Spaniards die on all sides, usually in an impressively acrobatic way.

I have to confess that we're a bit hazy on where and when the story takes place. I mean, at the start it does say **Casal 1630**, but that doesn't give us a lot to go on. We've wondered, we've discussed, we've debated. Given all the Spanish and French soldiers involved, it seems obvious Casal is in or near France or Spain (or potentially both). Though Hector raised the interesting possibility that it could be an actual country that doesn't exist any more. (We like this idea.) We're as shaky on dates as we are on geography. We've no idea what else was going on in the world in 1630, not a clue. For us history is made up of odd, brilliant, disconnected stories, against a background of dull bits. We pad it out a bit with stuff we read in books and comics and watch on television, and to be honest we're not always sure what really happened and what details we've added to make it more exciting. I wonder if that matters? We've agreed there are some advantages to not knowing. François and Guillot seem much more heroic out of time and place. They're pure heroes. And we want to be them.

I hear Lemur's intake of breath as François and Guillot are nearly caught by the Spanish soldiers. They leap onto their horses and gallop away just in time.

It's very busy, *The Flashing Blade,* with people arguing and fighting, all determined to find some way to either capture the castle or repel the attackers. You can't be totally sure who's telling the truth. There's a fair amount of double-dealing going on (and the dubbing can make all the characters seem a bit shifty). Even after a few repeats (and Kit, Bru, Skooshie, Hector and I are totally obsessed and reckon we've seen every episode at least three times, apart from the last one, which isn't shown very often and we've only managed to see once – *once!* – and even then the picture was rubbish and kept going fuzzy), we haven't quite grasped all of the reasons behind the different ploys each side uses. (To be honest, I have to make some of it up when Kit asks.)

But it's clear the Spanish are the bad guys and the French are the good guys. We know this because the French are outnumbered and are fighting against the odds and François and Guillot laugh in the face of this, while the Spaniards are arrogant and have no sense of humour. They also have ridiculous moustaches. I have a theory that those may slow them down when it comes to hand-to-hand combat, because the French usually win. The fights are brilliant! We are 100% behind François, even when he gets into trouble with his own side – because he's thinking for himself and doesn't do what he's told when he knows it's wrong. He's the best sword fighter by miles and is also really good at disguises – both very handy skills, as it turns out.

"THAT WAS FANTASTIC!" shouts Lemur, bouncing up and down on the cushions as Kit and I treat him to a rousing chorus of the song again while the closing credits roll up the screen. "Can I watch it with you again next time?"

"Yeah," I say. I'm very tempted to tell him that by episode two François will have been condemned to death *by his own side*, just to see the horror on Lemur's face. But a week's a long time to wait not knowing the outcome. I mean, *a week, a whole week* – it feels like torture to me and I already know what will happen! There's this brilliant bit when François is being taken away to prison and he says, "I surrender my sword to no man!" and he breaks his sword in two *on his knee* and throws away the pieces.

"Why have you never seen it before?" asks Kit. "Are you not allowed to watch it at home?"

Lemur looks embarrassed. "We don't have a television," he confesses.

That explains a lot.

"Why not?" asks Kit.

Lemur shrugs. "We just don't. Don't tell the others," he says to me.

"I think you should," I say. "They'll feel sorry for you. At the moment they just think you're weird."

In fact, I don't even give him the chance to think about it. As soon as we get into the den, I say, "Hey, guess what? Lemur hasn't got a telly!"

This is a technique of my dad's. No wee clues or hinting, no giving people time to work it out for themselves so they're not shocked. It's like ripping a plaster off your knee. You can do it slow and make the agony bearable but last for a long time or you can do it with one brutal yank that takes your breath away. But then it's done.

They suspect a wind-up at first. We don't know *anybody* who doesn't have a television! And when

Lemur tells them it is in fact true, Skooshie looks so sad for him I think he's going to take Lemur home to his already very full house and ask Mrs Skooshie to adopt him.

"So he's just seen his very first episode of *The Flashing Blade*!" I say.

"What did you think? Isn't François fantastic?" They fling questions at him without waiting for answers. Everybody's talking at once about their favourite bits. This goes on for some time until there's really nothing else to say. That happens just after Skooshie's asked, "What *is* a swash and what happens if you don't buckle it?" We decide it's time to go and do something else.

As always happens, one thing leads on to another and next thing we know, it's much too near the end of another sunny day. We're outside, on the patch of rough ground by Cathkin. We've been collecting dark purple berries. They're on a tree that's been allowed to seed and sprout inside Cathkin. Its neglected branches now tumble over the fence and the berries hanging heavily on them are easy to reach. They're small and a bit hard – we're not sure they are in fact ripe – but if you squash them you do get a pale purplish juice. We're using it to make wine.

None of us actually drinks it. We're not too sure about the berries but we're pretty confident that all the other stuff we've added will make us vomit, big time. We consider selling it but we haven't got enough cups.

Lemur's standing up at the fence. It's one of those mesh fences, where the wire is twisted into interlinked diamond shapes. Thousands and thousands of them.

The kind of pattern that makes your eyes go funny if you stare at it. He's twisted his fingers round the mesh and he's pushed his nose through one of the diamonds. Technically part of him is inside Cathkin. He looks round at us and we know exactly what he's going to say.

He grins. "I've got a plan."

I like Lemur's plans – we all do. He has pure dead brilliant ideas and the ones that aren't wild, illegal and/or lethal always turn out to be loads of fun. But the rest... Before the holidays, he tried to talk us into breaking into the Hampden Bowl, the abandoned bowling alley on Somerville Drive. And I mean *break in*. The place has no windows. We'd need actual equipment. He was all, "*C'mon* – let's do it!" If we don't watch him, he's going to land us in real trouble sometime.

6

What I've realised is that Lemur needs us – that his best plans are the ones that we've all helped shape: Hector with all his knowledge of weird and wonderful facts and his enthusiasm for planning; Bru with his ability to look at things from odd angles and ask the kind of questions that show up gaps in the thinking. Me, I think I'm good at coming up with alternative suggestions. And Skooshie? He crashes in, taking Lemur's ideas and making them crazier, until even Lemur can see we're sledging down a vertical mountain with no helmets and no brakes. At this point, if we're lucky, somebody will shout **WHOA!**, allowing us to tip ourselves sideways and sprawl in the snow catching our breath, while the sledge careers on down into the ravine...

So all I'm saying is that usually when Lemur says, "I've got a plan," it's time to start listening *very* carefully.

For Cathkin, what we need, as Hector says, is a plan devised and executed with military precision. A plan that is better than any other plan we've ever come up with. If we get caught, there will be no second chance. I will be kept in until I've done my Highers. "That I can guarantee," my mum has said. If you know her, you'll know she's not exaggerating.

From the sixth floor of our flats you can see everything. You can see anybody coming from or going into the back of the building. Any advancing armies (or unwelcome relatives), we know they're coming, no bother. The only weak spot is right up against the wall of the flats – anything slinking in that way you could only see if you loosened the safety catch on the window and leant out. That's not recommended – I know because I've gone close enough to see if it was do-able and there was hell to pay, believe me. Also, in our house we only have windows on two sides of the flats. So if people come in the front door, for example, you can't see them at all. I admit this would be quite a weakness in any serious attempt at defence.

Out the kitchen window you can see all the way to the West End. You can make out the tower of the university. And across the city more church spires than you can count. (Kit and I have tried: it has lead to arguments. She was so wrong.) And beyond the city, the Campsie Fells on the horizon. I like living high up. Not only is it always bright, even on quite cloudy days, and you can see what's going on, it also gives you a brilliant feeling of being truly Weegie, like the city's all yours. Who else is lucky enough to feel like this? Well, the people one floor up, maybe. And the ones on the sixth and seventh floors of the other flats, on the sides facing in the right direction. But you know what I mean. When I look out, I promise myself I will never live anywhere but here.

But the high-in-the-sky advantageous viewpoint can sometimes be an actual disadvantage. Out our living-room window, on the other side, is where you get a panoramic view of Cathkin. It's the stuff of cheering daydreams. You can stand and look, imagining the players shouting for the ball on the pitch and the crowds roaring on the terraces. But this prime location is what's causing us so many problems. Because doing Cathkin isn't just a question of getting past the corrugated metal put up to stop enterprising adventurers like us. The further we get into the park, the clearer the view my mum could have of us: dealing with *that* is the bigger challenge.

"It's a death-trap," she says. According to her, it would only take one of us to laugh too loudly for the whole roof of the abandoned stand to come crashing down on our heads. Or we'd trip on the unstable concrete (worn by time and smashed by hooligans), and tumble below the terracing, breaking a leg in the process (the leg wouldn't finish us off, but the starvation would, as we lay in the dank, dark hole, too weak to call for help). Or bogey men, waiting just for us, would jump out from their hiding places under the stand and carry us off. She doesn't say where to, just leaves you speculating, knowing that what you can think up is much, much worse than anything she can say... Oh, she's good, my mum.

But not quite as good as she thinks. Because with every word she says to me, she makes Cathkin more and more irresistible. We want to feel what it was like in its heyday: we want to run onto the pitch ready to do battle, like the players did. We want to lean on the crumbling concrete supports, and picture strikers running full pelt up the pitch and blasting the ball into the net in front of us. We want to risk the gloom of the stand, lying back and staring up at the rusting roof. We want to walk over every bit of broken concrete, challenging each other to find and leap the most dangerous gaps. We want to be players, managers, spectators, villains, heroes. It's the stage for so many possible adventures. It's calling out and we're the boys to answer it. We are desperate to get in there.

We fantasise about being the first, but accept the impossibility of this. Plenty of people have been there before us: we've heard them, sometimes spotted signs of them from my living-room window. When they first built the barrier round the whole park, abandoning it to thieves, vandals and natural rot, we were all about three. Plus our flats hadn't even been built. Some disappointments you just have to accept.

But now is our time. So there's a lot to organise. We have arguments about whether we should focus on identifying where to break in or on a plan to be invisible inside the park or on deciding what we'll do when we get there. It usually ends with everybody talking, nobody listening and nothing being decided. Which is getting us exactly nowhere. We're counting down. There are *two days* before we go in. So this time when Lemur turns to us, saying with so much confidence that he's got a plan, I say, "Let's hear it then." And even before I hear it, I'm thinking, "Let's do it!"

"Let's find somewhere safe we can talk," says Hector.

We're sitting on the grass, above the steps to Prospecthill
Road. From here we see anybody approaching from
any direction. Hector chose the place. We're listening
to Lemur.

"Where *exactly*?" I ask, unable to believe my ears.

"The bit right – under – your – living – room –
window," he says triumphantly.

"Are you mad?"

"No. Look. We've talked about getting in behind
the stand. That does give the best cover – you can't
see there from your house. But – and it's a big but – we
would have to walk halfway round the outside of the
park to get there."

"We'd be spotted for sure," Hector says.

"Exactly," says Lemur. "Whereas, if we slip in behind
the corrugated iron opposite, we only run the risk of
being seen for a minute."

"But we'll be seen as soon as we're up the embankment
inside – you can see *everything* from our house."

"But we're not climbing the embankment," says
Lemur. "We're going to go *along the bottom of it*."

"He's right, Midge," says Bru. "It's all overgrown
there. It'll hide us."

"We go right round, most of the way to the stand.
There's an open bit between the terracing and the stand.
We'll need to sprint that."

"It might work," I say grudgingly. I'm up for it – I just
don't want Lemur getting all the glory. "Wait a minute

– how loose is the corrugated iron? Are you sure we can just pull it open?"

We screw up our eyes and look down the hill, trying to form a judgement. Not being owls, we're defeated by the dark and the distance.

Then we hear somebody trundling the front door of our flats open. My dad gives us a wave as he heads off down the road to the lighting depot. He's working nightshift this week, so he's carrying his flask and his cheese pieces wrapped up in tinfoil. I run down to see him.

"Ten minutes, son. Then up, OK?"

"OK, Dad. See you in the morning."

"See you, son. See you, lads."

"Just enough time to check out the iron barrier," says Bru, once my dad's out of sight. He jumps to his feet. Lemur pulls him back down. "No. We don't want to risk it. A big crowd of us gathering round there – we might be spotted. I'll check it out on my way home."

"No, let Hector go," I say. "You've already looked at it, Lemur. A second opinion's what we need."

Hector's up and off before Lemur can object. He gives us a grin and a salute and disappears into the gloaming. "I'll report back tomorrow!"

The rest of us get up, reluctantly. "See youse," says Skooshie, with a sigh. At times like these we would give anything we own or are ever likely to own just to stay out playing. Where's that Time Bank when we need it?

I'm obviously more berry stained than I realised, because when I go up, the first thing my mum says is, "Bath!"

"I'm not sure I have the energy," I tell her. "I might drown."

"Bath!"

When I go to bed at night, I'm asleep before my head even hits the pillow. But in the morning the light wakes me early. And as I lie there, I can't not think about school sometimes. I think about knowing nobody. I think about the fact half of them will know each other, because they went to the same primary school. I think about all the new subjects and teachers. And it's exciting – really exciting – but I'm scared as well. Don't think I'm worried about not being clever enough – I think I can handle that. I just can't imagine what it will feel like to fit in, in a place that has no Lemur, no Hector, no Skoosh, no Bru.

They don't blame me, I don't think they do. Our teacher said Bru and Hector should try too, and Hector did and he got in as well but then he said he wasn't going. Bru's mum and dad didn't think it was worth Bru trying.

So it's just me.

7

Hector turns up the next morning with the worst possible news. The corrugated iron isn't loose enough. So tomorrow is *not* Cathkin Day.

"Ah," says Skooshie knowingly. "What we need is a jemmy."

"A what?"

"A jemmy. It's a metal pole with a flat end – we'll use it to prise the iron sheet away from the fence."

"Where're we going to get *that*?"

"Can you buy them?"

"They're *really* expensive."

"So who'd have one?"

"Don't know – a burglar, maybe."

"Anybody know any burglars?"

"Well, there's Skooshie's Uncle Harry..."

"Just watch it, Lemur!"

"I'm joking!"

We were all looking at Skooshie up till this point (as clearly he's the nearest to an expert in the jemmy area that we've got), but we look away in a hurry now, not wanting him to think that we were thinking about his Uncle Harry too. I'm not trying to suggest *anything* about Skooshie's Uncle Harry or his occupation. I've met him and he's really nice. He gave us money for sweets.

Skooshie grunts. It's the kind of grunt that means he's not offended. "Leave it with me. I *might* know where to find one. It could take a while, though."

So we settle on that as Plan B (presuming we're not counting the other 278 plans that came before Lemur's Plan A). This still leaves us with an empty day.

"Time to consult The List," says Hector. He reads it out loud, pausing for us to respond after each suggestion.

"Football."

"Done that."

"Tennis."

"Naaa."

"Queen's Park."

"Not today."

"Scavy hunt?"

We just sigh.

"Games/Competitions."

A collective groan.

"Invent Time Bank."

"Yeah, right."

"It's a good list," I say. "This just felt like a day for planning something... bigger."

"Yeah."

And there we were, slumped on the old settee cushions, not an ounce of energy between us. And we might be there still, if Hector, in an effort to drum up some enthusiasm, hadn't started whistling *The Flashing Blade* theme tune.

"*That's it!*" shouts Lemur, jumping up.

We look at him, slightly hopeful but unwilling to move until we know for certain it's worth it.

"It *is* a day for planning something bigger," he says. "The time has come for Mrs Whistle-Blower Revenge!"

This is enough to fire Skooshie up. "REVENGE!" he shouts.

"*Revenge?*" says Hector.

"Revenge," I say firmly. "I'm absolutely totally bored enough for revenge, whatever the risks."

"C'mon, Hector. You know you want to..." says Lemur with a grin.

And next thing we're all quizzing Bru for any intell from his Mrs WB encounter that will help us come up with a plan.

"Was it like the entrance to a witch's coven – all dark and cobwebby, with great big spiders and loads of wee vampire bats hanging down?"

"No," says Bru, regretfully. "It looked just like our doors except that she's got a big flowerpot outside."

"Those big, scary man-eating flowers – what d'y'call them?"

"Venus flytraps."

"There to trap unwary boys..." says Skooshie, snapping carnivorously.

"Funnily enough, they weren't boy-eating Venus flytraps, Skooshie," says Bru. "They were plastic roses – and I know that because..."

"Start at the beginning," Hector interrupts. "Don't miss anything out."

"Did you have to go inside?"

"What if she'd just kept you prisoner in her house, to teach the rest of us a lesson?"

"Did she have the whistle on a cord round her neck?"

"No, I didn't have to go inside – which was a relief. She was all scowly and peering at me through her glasses while I said my bit about being sorry."

"Sorry that you've got such an annoying wee brother!"

"Sorry that she's deaf!"

"And then she had a go. Children these days – no respect – thoughtlessness – you'll be old one day. She kept talking that long, I didn't think she'd ever finish. I started to wonder if anybody had ever been talked to death – if I might just petrify like those trees in Scotstoun Park, buried and turned to stone under the relentless pressure of Mrs Whistle-Blower's voice."

"Why didn't you just leave?" asks Lemur.

"I didn't want to make it worse. I'd just have had to come back when she told on me again. So eventually she finished but I didn't know she had and I was still standing there like a numpty. She flicked her hand at me in an away-you-go-you-small-boy gesture, and I turned round a bit sharpish and kicked over her flowerpot."

"Oooof!"

"That's how I know about the flowers being plastic. I did think she completely over-reacted, considering I hadn't killed it. I put it the right way up and gave it a wee dust, then I legged it."

"The flowerpot!" says Lemur. "There's our revenge!"

"Oh-oh," says Hector. I know what he means. Lemur's got that look in his eye, the one he gets when he's leading us right into trouble.

"We're going to steal her flowerpot!" Lemur announces.

Hector raises his eyebrows. Bru and I exchange a hopeful glance that says, "Aw, could we?" Skooshie whoops with delight.

"C'mon, Hector," says Lemur. "You know she deserves it. And it's the only thing we can get to."

"I don't know," says Hector. "Nicking stuff – it's not right."

"Well... we won't take it for good," says Lemur.

"Really? You promise?"

"Yes," says Lemur with a grin. "She'll get it back in time. We just want to keep it long enough to wind her up."

"So you're on for it, Hector?" asks Bru.

"I'm on – as long as we return it once she's good and annoyed."

"And she won't ever know it was us," says Lemur.

I wonder briefly what the chances are of this being true. You'll find out soon enough.

So Hector officially changes The List, adding in huge letters WBFPR (Whistle-Blower's Flowerpot Removal), known in all future discussions as "Wibfipper". Apart from that, we don't see much of his usual enthusiasm for planning. It's like he's still a bit doubtful about the whole enterprise.

"Let's do it now!" says Skooshie.

"Too much chance of other people seeing us with the flowerpot," I say. "I mean, boys coming out of those flats carrying a pot of plastic flowers. It's going to look suspicious."

"Maybe we could have a back-up story ready?" says Lemur.

"What like?"

"Like we're from a flowerpot repair company," says Skooshie.

"Yes," says Lemur. "That Bru broke it a bit when he kicked it—"

"I did not!" Bru is outraged at the unfairness of the suggestion.

"I know, I know... I'm just saying, it would be a good excuse – that we were all there taking it away to be fixed. Like they do with televisions."

"(1)," Hector interrupts loudly, in the tone of a man unable to bear the havering any longer, "there's no such thing as a flowerpot repair company. (2) Even if there was, it wouldn't employ twelve-year-old boys. And (3) even if it did, how big is the flowerpot that it would need five of us – five of us! – to carry it?"

"It's not that big a flowerpot," Bru confirms.

"Hector's right," says Lemur. He looks into the distance and sighs, then says, "What do *you* think we should do, Hector?"

I glance at Lemur in surprise. Is this Lemur *handing over control* to Hector? Is that pigs oinking overhead that I can hear? Will I get home tonight to find a single Jammy Dodger left in the biscuit tin and hear Kit say, "No, Midge, I think *you* should have it." Lemur catches my eye and winks.

"We need two men in there at most – any more and we'll definitely get caught," says Hector. Looks like he's warming to the plan now. "One to get the pot, the other to watch out for anybody coming. The rest stay outside and give warning if anybody's coming into the flats."

"We can bark like a dog!"

"We could," says Hector. "Though as dogs aren't actually allowed in the flats that might stand out a bit. Why don't we do a bird call?"

We pool our knowledge. It turns out we know owl, seagull and crow. To be honest, our seagulls and our crows sound much the same. Bru can do a sparrow, but that's ruled out as too quiet. We're all really good at owl. Then Hector points out it's a night bird.

"We could go for the flowerpot just as it's getting dark?" suggests Lemur. "There won't be many people coming in and out of the flats, so as long as we're quiet we shouldn't be noticed."

"And any hooting will blend right in at that time of day," Bru adds.

"Owl it is," says Hector. "So about half past eight?... Good. Any volunteers for the actual Wibfippering?"

Skooshie's hand shoots up, like he's still at school. "Me!"

"Bru should probably lie low on this one," says Lemur.

"Why?" Bru demands.

"The whole Kenny fiasco, Bru," I say. "You'll be top of any suspects list she makes. Just in case."

"Aw, right – good point."

"You and me then, Skoosh," says Lemur.

"Good – so Lemur and Skooshie on the inside. Bru, Midge and me covering the outside. You'll need to take a bag for the flowerpot – a dark bag, so you blend in. I think we might have one at home."

Hector in charge – Hector in his element.

"Time to practise our own calls!" he concludes.

"Whooo, whooo, whooo's ready for revenge?"

"WE ARE!"

8

We're sitting outside Mrs Whistle-Blower's flats, waiting, Bru, Hector and me. We knew we couldn't get too close or any old folk looking out their windows would see us and jump unreasonably to the conclusion we were up to no good. So we hide ourselves behind the lock-ups, within hooting distance. We take turns peeking round the corner to keep an eye on the front entrance.

"This is really boring," says Bru.

"It's important," says Hector. "They can't complete their mission without us in place here."

"We should have risked it," says Bru. "We should all have gone in."

"Playing with fire."

Bru sighs. "I'd've liked the satisfaction of nicking her stupid flowers."

"*What's that*?" hisses Hector.

"Two old blokes coming out," I say, because it's my turn to be surveillance guy. "It's fine – they're heading for the pub."

"How did you work that one out, Sherlock?"

"Well, it's half past eight so the shops are shut – and they look happy," I say. "Plus I overheard one of them saying, 'Tommy said he'll see us down the pub at nine.'"

"Excellent detective work," says Bru. "Is it my turn now?"

We wait. Nothing happens. I consider trying a hoot, just to see whether I'll be loud enough if I need to make the call. I decide it's not worth the grief Hector will give me.

"D'you not think I should just go and make sure they're OK?" asks Bru.

Hector doesn't get the chance to answer. The front door of the flats is flung open, and Lemur and Skooshie come pelting towards us. There are yellow flowers sprouting out of Lemur's armpit and Hector's bag is flapping in Skooshie's hand.

They don't stop.

"*RUN!*" shouts Skooshie as they career past us.

We're sitting in the den in a circle round the loot. With a dramatic gesture, Lemur pulls the bag off and throws it to one side – "TA DA!" – to reveal a small brown pot with some yellow plastic roses in it. We're not that impressed because we saw them before Lemur put them under the bag so he could do his ta-da gesture.

"The spoils of war!" he says, triumphant.

"Tell us what happened," I say. "It felt like we were waiting for ages. What took you so long?"

"We had to be really careful," says Lemur. "We slipped in at the back of the flats, just as planned."

"We'd just got in when we heard the lift coming down," says Skooshie. "So we had to hide in the bit under the stairs till they'd gone."

"Yeah, we saw them coming out from our vantage point," says Hector. "Two old guys going to the pub, we reckoned – no threat, so no hooting."

"Then we started creeping up the stairs..."

"Slowly, slowly, not making any noise..."

"Not breathing too loud..."

"Not giggling..."

"I do not *giggle*," says Skooshie. "*Girls* giggle. I... snort."

"Not snorting..."

"Well, trying *really hard* not to snort..." Skooshie admits.

"Until we got to the right floor. We opened the first door..." Here Lemur pauses dramatically, "which creaks like the entrance to Dracula's castle!"

"*EEEEEEKKKKKKKKKRRRRRREEEEEEE...*"

"We stop. We wait. We listen."

"We're wondering: what do we do?"

"Do we continue with the plan, taking it slowly?"

"Just hoping that she didn't hear the house-of-horror sound effect?"

"Or do we speed it up – get in, get the pot, get out?"

"You changed the plan?" says Hector accusingly. "Without telling us?"

"Well, Hector, it turned out I'm not as fluent as I thought," says Skooshie. "I didn't know the Owl for 'Hector, Hector, please send us an emergency change of plan by hoot!'"

"We had to think on our feet," says Lemur. "It just

made sense at the time. So Skooshie pulled open the second door—"

"Really quick, like pulling out a baby tooth."

"I jumped in, grabbed the flowers—"

"Out the squeaky door – *EEEEEEKKKKKKKKRR*—"

"Thanks, Skoosh. I think we got the idea the first time."

"Then down the stairs as fast as we could."

"But really quietly down the stairs?" I say.

"Kind of."

"You were supposed to do it really really quietly, so they didn't come out of their flats and see you!" says Hector.

"No one came out," says Lemur.

"So why were you running?"

"It was more exciting," Skooshie admits.

"Well, mission accomplished, I suppose," says Hector, grudgingly. Then he grins at the sight of the flowers. "Do you feel avenged, Bru?"

"I do, Hector, I do. It would be even better if I could see her face when she finds out they're gone."

"Well, that might be possible," says Lemur.

"What?"

"I've had a really good idea..."

"Lemur, we are still taking them back?" says Hector. It's half a statement and half a question because Lemur has a gleeful look in his eyes.

"Well... this idea is better."

"Lemur – you said! We all agreed we wouldn't keep it!"

"Though it does look quite good in here," says Skooshie. "As a trophy," he adds when we all look at him. "It's not that I'm wanting flowers in the den. Girls stuff – yuk."

"I didn't say we'd take it back," says Lemur.

"You did!"

"No – I said she'd *get it* back."

"What are you thinking, Lemur?" Bru asks. "I'm definitely being involved in this bit. Nobody's going to stop me."

"Well, I could tell you," says Lemur. "But I think it will be funnier if you wait until tomorrow morning and see for yourself. Apart from you, Bru. You're going to help me. *C'mon!*"

9

We agreed to meet the next morning outside my flats, early. It's so early nobody's up bar the milkman and the postman. We're the only kids out. Bru didn't walk home with me the evening before, so I didn't get the chance to discuss with him what Lemur was up to. I'm desperate to find out.

Hector and Skooshie are the first to arrive. We sit on the steps, trying to guess Lemur's plan.

"Maybe he and Bru are going to return it to her, like they found it after it was stolen and thought she'd like it back," says Hector. "Then we'd be in her good books."

Skooshie and I both screw up our faces in disbelief. I'm tempted to do a (1), (2) list of reasons why Hector is so wrong, but it's too early and I can't be bothered.

"Not Lemur's style," is all I say.

"True," Hector agrees.

Bru appears from his flats and we see Lemur coming down the hill at about the same time.

"This way," says Lemur.

He takes us the long way round to Mrs Whistle-Blower's flats.

"Here," he says, sitting down in a shady bit and leaning back against the wall behind.

We copy him and find we have the ideal view. Not only of Mrs Whistle-Blower's window, but also of Mrs Whistle-Blower's flowerpot, which has somehow found its way onto the roof of the lock-ups. It stands out against the sky, looking quite grand and totally inaccessible. Which is how Mrs Whistle-Blower finds it when she opens her curtains five minutes later. We are perfectly placed to see the shocked expression on her face – just before she turns away from the window in a hurry.

"Quick," says Lemur. "She's gone to look outside her door to check if her flowers are missing."

We take the opportunity to slink off.

"Lemur, I've got an idea for what to do next," I say.

"But we're done," says Lemur. "Wasn't it the best ending?"

"The look on her face was priceless," says Bru. "I loved it!"

"I think it can be even better," I say.

An hour later things are a bit livelier – more kids are up and out playing. There's the usual soundtrack of squealing and laughing and yelling, balls bouncing and skipping-ropes slapping the tarmac. Cue Part Two of the plan.

"We'll need the tennis racquets," I say.

"To start an argument with her?" says Skooshie.

"Don't you think we'd be better avoiding her, in case she suspects us?" asks Hector.

"No – we'll just look guilty if we don't act normal." And I fill them in on what's going to happen.

We stroll casually down to Mrs Whistle-Blower's flats, racquets in hand. Hector is bouncing a ball up in the air off his – "One – two – three – four..." – like he hasn't another thought in the world.

"Topspin," says Bru out of nowhere. "It's all about the topspin." And I realise he's Acting Normal. She's at the window, looking at us.

I hear her open the window. She shouts down, "You boys!"

We look around as though startled. Who could be calling us? We locate where the voice is coming from, squinting up into the sun and using our hands to shade our eyes and our guilty expressions.

"Yes, you!"

"We were just going to play tennis against this wall, Mrs," says Skooshie, in a mildly aggrieved tone.

"But if it's too noisy, we can go somewhere else," says Lemur, helpfully.

"No – no, it's not that," she says.

I want to laugh out loud. Having to turn down our offer to go away – how exasperating must that feel! She has practically invited us to play a noisy ballgame right under her window.

"You see those flowers?" she says.

Flowers? We look around, surprised, amazed, confused – flowers, in the middle of all this concrete?

"There! There!" she says, gesturing impatiently in the direction of the lock-ups.

Oh! We fake astonishment in more or less

convincing ways. Skooshie overdoes it, staggering backwards as though the sight of four plastic yellow roses above his head is too much for him. Lemur grabs him, managing to stand painfully hard on his foot at the same time, to bring him to his senses. Skooshie yelps.

"Sorry, Skoosh. Did I trip you there?"

"Those flowers up there?" I say.

"Yes, those flowers! Would one of you boys go up onto the roof and get them for me? They're mine."

"No bother." Hector thrusts his racquet at me, and next second he's clambering up onto the roof.

"What are they doing up there?" Skooshie says to no one in particular.

Mrs Whistle-Blower ignores him. We shrug and make *pffff* noises, showing just how puzzled we are.

Hector appears at the edge of the lock-up roof and picks up the flowers in their pot very carefully, like they're fragile. He looms above us, grinning down.

"Got them!" he calls to Mrs Whistle-Blower. "Do you want me to bring them up to you?"

"That would be very helpful." She closes her window. We keep in character, knowing that she's still watching. We clap Hector on the back, like he's just rescued a drowning puppy.

"All of us?" asks Bru.

"Oh, I think so," says Lemur.

"But you at the back, Bru," says Hector. "Just in case she recognises you and makes the connection."

"What connection?"

"With a boy who had it in for her flowers before."

She seems quite taken aback at the sight of all five of us, crammed into the small hall outside her door.

"Here you are!" says Hector, thrusting the flowerpot at her. "I think they enjoyed their outing – they're looking quite fresh."

She eyes him suspiciously. "Thank you," she says.

We don't move. She looks at us. We stand, smiling expectantly.

"Wait here a minute," she orders. She closes the door, taking the flowerpot with her. We wait. A minute later she opens the door again.

"Here you are."

She thrusts five biscuits at Hector and closes the door with a loud and definitive click.

We troop down the stairs, keeping our glee in check until we get somewhere safe. Skooshie's the only one to speak.

"Not even chocolate ones," he says, taking a disappointed bite. "After all we did for her."

10

Well, would you believe it, Wipfipper turns out not to be our only close encounter with oldsters that week. A few days later I'm standing in front of the lift watching the **CAR COMING** sign. It's lit orange to say the lift is on its way down, coming from the very top floor. The numbers light up slowly in turn – **7, 6, 5** ... So slowly that more than once I think the lift's got stuck. It's only that slow when I'm in a hurry.

"Anytime, Mr Murphy," my mum is saying. "Anytime you need anything, you just let us know. If you need anything from the shops – a newspaper, bread – James can get it for you."

That gets my attention. It's an old man she's talking to. He's wearing a brown coat, even though it's quite warm, and a red and white scarf. "That's kind of you," he's saying. He doesn't seem very chatty, but then my mum doesn't always leave much opportunity for other people to get a word in.

She's off again, this time telling him about my new school. I really hate it when she does this.

"James is off to the Grammar in August. He did well

in the exam. He had to do a lot of preparation for it – his teacher was very, very good, really supported him. He'll need to work hard there, we've been telling him. Haven't we, James?"

"Yes," I say, my eyes glued on the lift numbers. I've found that the best way is not to get into a conversation – if you're lucky, she then just talks her way into a new topic and no one's offended. I glance at the old man to work out just how bored he is by my educational history. Unseen by my mum, he gives me half a smile and a complicit wink, as if to say "Mothers, eh?"

I can hear them before the door at the back of the flats is pushed open on its runner. I silently beg my mum not to talk about the Grammar. For once my telepathic message works. Hector, Lemur, Skooshie and Bru tumble in and there's a noisy exchange of hiya's. Then there's a pause: they don't quite understand why I am there but not coming with them.

"I just need James to help me up with these bags, boys," says my mum. "We've been to the shops. Then he's all yours."

"Thanks, Mrs Laird," says Hector. "Good job you're back, Midge – lots on today." He gives me a knowing nod, which is supposed to be a secret sign between us that we will be discussing our Cathkin plan. If he had made a poster saying WE'RE UP TO NO GOOD and stuck it on the side of the local bus shelter, he could not have made it clearer to my mum. She pretends not to notice.

"What's your plan?" asks Mr Murphy, surprising us all by his interest.

"Football," Bru says, before Hector can give away anything more. "Training for a very important game."

"Yeah," says Skooshie, getting into it. "Need to be fit." He throws his elbows high and wide in a muscle-building move – and catches Lemur right in the chest.

"OW!" Lemur lashes out at Skooshie with his one free hand. The other hand is clutching at his chest, like an internal organ might fall out if he doesn't. We all know that if my mum wasn't there, this offence of Skooshie's would justify a full-scale fight.

Mr Murphy laughs. "You might want to practise that one away from your pals. Are you all right there?"

"Yes." Lemur glares at Skooshie. "I'm fine – but he's a lunatic!"

And when Lemur speaks, Mr Murphy looks at him as if he hasn't really noticed him before. Then he pushes Skooshie out of the way and grabs Lemur by the arm.

"It's *you*," he says. "I know it's you."

Lemur tries to pull himself out of the old man's grip.

"Give it back. *JUST GIVE ME IT BACK!*" Mr Murphy is shouting now.

"What?" Lemur tries to pull away but the old man holds on fiercely.

"You – have – to – give – me – it – back!" With each word, Mr Murphy shakes Lemur.

Two things happen at once. The lift door opens revealing Kit and her friend Shelagh. And my mum says, *"Mr Murphy! Let him alone!"* in a voice she usually keeps for giving me the most deadly serious kind of row. For a second, everything freezes, then the lift doors start to close and Kit jumps forward to press the **HOLD** button. She absolutely does not want to miss any of this performance.

Mr Murphy steps back, dropping Lemur's arm. He touches his head. He looks confused and unsure of himself. Lemur has turned pure white.

"I'm sorry, I'm sorry," says Mr Murphy. "He looked just like... I was thinking you were somebody else, another lad... I'm very sorry. I'm sorry."

The lift doors start to close again. I put my foot in to stop them. The last thing we need is to wait here until it goes up and comes back down again. Kit and Shelagh have got out. My mum and Mr Murphy get in. I don't.

"There's not enough room for us all, Mum. We'll walk up the stairs!"

Lemur is the first to escape. We lug the shopping bags up all twelve flights to the sixth floor. I have to stop on the way for a rest. Lemur doesn't want to pause. "C'mon – we're nearly there."

"We're not nearly there," I protest. "We're only halfway up. Wait just a minute."

We're too breathless to say what we are all thinking – *What was that about?* Or maybe we don't talk because we know we can be heard by anybody further up, anybody crossing the stair landing on the way from the lift to their flat.

By the time we get into my house, my dad has already been told the whole story. Maybe more than once.

"I didn't even realise it was him at first," says my mum. "I was looking at the lift numbers. I thought it was one of you lot messing about. Are you all right, eh... Lemur?"

Lemur nods. "But a biscuit might help," he croaks weakly.

My dad laughs. "Nice move, son. What about your posse? D'you think they need biscuits for the shock too?"

"And carrying the bags up the stairs, Mr Laird," says Bru.

"He just lost it, Dad," I say as we sit munching.

"He kept going on about wanting something back," says my mum.

"Did he?" says Bru. "I don't think he was that clear – it all sounded a bit garbled to me."

"He's one that'll need to be sent back to the Glasgow Corporation Old Folks' Factory for repair," says my dad.

"I wonder what his problem is?" Skooshie dips a finger into his Tunnock's Tea Cake to scoop out the marshmallow. "You can't just go around accusing innocent people."

"Old people sometimes get a bit confused," says my mum, her forehead crinkling with hard thinking – or possibly disgust at Skooshie's table manners. "He did look very upset. I'll pop up and see him later, when it's all calmed down."

"Really?" I say. "Is that a good idea, Mum?"

"Why not?"

"Well, if he did get confused, you'll make him feel bad if you remind him about it," I say. "You'll make it seem a bigger deal than it was."

Hector nods and pauses in his crunching to say, "Good point, Midge."

My mum doesn't seem to think so. She can never ever

resist finding out the whole story. And there's something in the way she glances at Lemur when he helps himself to another Jaffa Cake that worries me. But I can't risk saying any more. And as it becomes clear that there are no more biscuits on offer, we leave.

Back in the den, my mum and dad out of the picture, no one has to pretend any more.

"So, Lemur. What did you nick from Mr Murphy?"

"It was more than a flowerpot – nobody gets that excited about a flowerpot."

"You actually went and did it without us?"

"I don't even know where he lives!" Lemur protests. "Honest, I didn't steal his flowerpot – or his newspaper – or his hat – or his dog!"

"His dog? He doesn't have a dog!"

"He doesn't have a dog *now*."

"So where *is* the dog, Lemur?"

"*There is no dog*, Skooshie!"

Lemur holds out his hands. "Stop! Listen to me. The whole Wibfipper adventure – why did we do it?"

"REVENGE!" shouts Skooshie.

"Exactly!" says Lemur. "We did it for a reason. Tell me, what's my reason for stealing anything from that old man? And also tell me why I'd do it on my own, when we're a team?"

"He's got a point," says Hector.

"Oh, no," groans Bru with real feeling.

"What?"

"If Lemur *didn't* steal anything from Mr Murphy, it means Mr Murphy must know what we did to Mrs Whistle-Blower. Aw, we're in real trouble!"

"How could he know? Could he have seen us?"

"Where does he live, Midge?"

"On the floor above – right above our house."

"No way he could see Mrs WB's flats from his window."

"Did he see you two putting the flowers on the lock-up?"

"No – it was really dark when we did it."

"Mrs WB worked it out – and she told him!"

"We're being kept in for the rest of the summer, for definite!"

"Aw, no Cathkin..."

"Wait a minute," I say. "Stop panicking! (1) He was going on about getting something back. Well, she's got her flowers. (2) If she did think it was us, she wouldn't waste time telling anybody else – she'd go straight to our parents. (3) If he knew, why didn't he just tell my mum?"

"That's true..."

"So the old bloke did just flip?"

"Looks like it."

"Is his house *right* above you, Midge?" asks Skooshie. "Right above your head?"

"Yeah."

"Ooof!" says Hector. "Rather you than me!"

"So when you're lying in bed asleep at night, he could just drop through the ceiling and attack you!"

"Yeah, Skooshie – I lie awake worrying about that.

I listen out for the sound of a saw and try to work out how to defend myself against somebody who's about 150 years old."

"Well," says Bru. "I'm thinking you should use kung fu as a first resort."

He crouches in a defensive stance ready to demonstrate. I jump into position opposite him.

"Remember," he continues. "Hurt, but do not kill, Glasshoppa. For life is plecious."

He loses his balance and his Chinese accent when my swift kick to the bum has him sprawling on the floor.

I help him up. Hands together, we bow to each other. "Thank you, Master."

When I get undressed for bed, I forget to consider the danger that Mr Murphy might drop down through the ceiling. I'm thinking about a caterpillar I've just found in my sock. It's not looking too lively. I give it a wee poke but it doesn't respond. So I put it on the windowsill in case it's just a bit shy or shell-shocked and not actually dead.

In the morning, the caterpillar's gone. Which is good. I don't bother telling Kit about it. She's funny about creepy-crawlies. So it's lucky we live this high up. Very few of them have the stamina for the journey.

11

Things quieten down a bit after this. My mum does go and see Mr Murphy, and apparently he's totally embarrassed and can't shut his door quick enough. No more accusations from him. It looks like we're in the clear as far as Wibfipper goes, but after a lot of debate we decide it would be wise to keep a low profile just for a few days. Which means passing on this Friday for Cathkin – no point in tempting fate. Our continuing lack of a jemmy means we don't really have much choice anyway. So, if the jemmy turns up, it's to be next week. Every so often we'll ask, "How's the search going, Skooshie?" And he'll respond by tapping the side of his nose and scrunching his eyes mysteriously as he says, "Ask me no questions and I'll tell you no lies," or "Good things come to those who wait," or some other annoying piece of pish. I'm starting to wonder if he talks like this just for the pleasure of seeing Lemur pushed to the point of desperation.

All the waiting is driving me mad too. Kit senses that something is up. I think I've told you before that she's nosy? Really, you've no idea... Give her the tiniest, toatiest hint there's something you're not telling her and she grabs it and hangs on like a ferret.

"It's Lemur, isn't it?"

"What's Lemur?"

"That you're thinking about. Mr Murphy giving him a hard time."

"That was ages ago!"

"But you're still thinking about it. I know you are. Is it because you think Mr Murphy didn't make a mistake?"

"*What?*"

"That he really *did* recognise Lemur. What was it he said? 'Give it back!'"

"You sounded just like Benny out of *Top Cat* when you did Mr Murphy there."

"Don't try and change the subject. You know what I think?"

"No. And I don't really care."

"I think Lemur might actually have stolen something from Mr Murphy!"

"Really? You should definitely be a detective."

"You think you know everything that Lemur does? You've said before that he's always got loads of plans and you don't always go along with them because they're so crazy."

"So?"

"So he might just have got fed up with that and done something on his own."

"He wouldn't do that."

"I wonder if he's going to get into trouble? Big trouble? That's what's worrying you, isn't it?"

"Oh, Kit, shut up."

"Does he get annoyed with the rest of you being big wusses? D'you think he'd like to be in a different gang?"

"No! He's one of us. Always."

"But different from the rest of you?"

"No. Not really. Well, he kind of is, kind of – but not really. In fact, he's just like all of us."

"How?"

"Well, he's like Hector in that he..."

"Is a know-all."

"...knows a lot of stuff and he likes to be in charge. He's daring like Skoosh – always up for a new adventure."

"How's he like Bru?"

"Well, he's really loyal. You can totally trust him."

"Until the Mr Murphy incident..."

"Don't you ever get tired of the sound of your own voice?"

"Never."

"You can *absolutely* trust Lemur."

"Can they not trust you?"

"That's not what I meant. I just mean it's a particular characteristic."

"And I suppose he's like you because he's clever and funny?"

"You admit I'm clever and funny?"

"Only compared to your friends. Not compared to normal people."

I throw a cushion at her head. It's the only way to stop her prattling sometimes.

Still, at least I know she suspects nothing about Cathkin.

The days get hotter and hotter. Skooshie, Hector and I are turning brown – and not all of it's dirt. Lemur and Bru don't really tan. Well, maybe Bru does. With his freckles, it's a bit hard to tell – they might be a bit more joined up than usual. Lemur stays as white as a pint of milk. I roll out of bed every morning sure it will be sunny and it is. I grab the nearest pair of shorts and the first clean t-shirt in the drawer. I pull on my sandshoes while I'm chewing my toast. If I'm caught before getting to the door, I brush my teeth. Bed to outside in less than ten minutes.

So one morning – it was the Thursday before Cathkin Friday (yes, that close) – I'm sitting on the grass near the flats waiting for everybody to arrive when Skooshie turns up. He's walking really oddly, like he can't bend. He's also got his arm glued to his side. Unusually in this heat, he's wearing long football socks. Even more unusually, they're pulled right up over his knees, nearly reaching his shorts.

"Are you expecting snow, Skoosh?" I'm about to ask, but I'm stopped by his curious expression. He's rolling his eyes up really high, then down towards his glued arm. He looks like a toad who hasn't yet learned how to catch flies successfully.

"What are you doing?"

"*I've got it,*" he hisses, still doing the eye-rolling thing.

It's only then that I notice, in the small gap between the top of his socks and the hem of his shorts, a dark piece of metal. The jemmy! It's well concealed – jammed up his t-shirt and down his socks – which goes a long way to explaining the funny walking.

"*Brilliant!*" I hiss back. "Why have you brought it here? How did you get down all the stairs?"

"It took a while," he confesses. "But Hector thought it would be better to hide it by the fence – so we're quicker tomorrow."

"Good plan."

"You all right, son?" Mrs Clarke from our flats has appeared, shopping bag over her arm. She's looking at Skooshie with concern. "I saw you coming down the stairs there. Is your leg really sore?"

"He was just practising, Mrs Clarke," I say. "We're competing in a three-legged race and he's so keen, he started training on his own."

"Aw, right... I'm glad you're OK."

We decide the safest thing is to hide the jemmy inside Cathkin. I cover while Skooshie extracts it from his sock and slots it in under the iron fence, within easy reach of anybody who know it's there but totally hidden from the rest of the world. He picks a dock leaf while he's down there and applies it to a fictional jaggy nettle sting in his hand as he stands up, just in case anybody should be watching and wondering what he's doing rummaging in the undergrowth.

We go back to wait for the others to arrive. We sit in the sun and talk about just how brilliant Cathkin's going to be.

Once they come we play tennis against the wall, measuring and marking a net. There's been tennis on the television so we're in the mood. We take it in turn to play, partly to make it competitive and partly because we only have three racquets between us. Bru wonders if we should maybe call it squash, but none of us is really sure what squash is. We've never known of anybody who's actually played it. But tennis we love. Bru's convinced he's Jimmy Connors – he never gives up even when it's hopeless. Lemur puts on a Borg-like coolness, not reacting even at his best shots. Once he tried falling on his knees when he beat us all, but tarmac is a lot tougher on the knees than grass. He won't be doing *that* again in a hurry.

Today we've got to the best wall before any girls show up to get in the way with their skipping games and their prams and their dolls. Bru, Skooshie and I are sitting on the steps in the shade, watching a tough final between Lemur and Hector.

"My money's on Hector," says Bru.

"No chance," I say. "Lemur's tanking him."

Play stops briefly while the players debate whether Lemur's last shot was actually below the net.

"FAULT!" shouts Skooshie. He points a warning finger at them to head off any argument. "The umpire's decision is *final*."

Play resumes. A wild ricochet on the next shot propels the ball past both of them. It's bouncing down the hill towards the road. Lemur and Hector look hopefully in our direction. We shrug and shake our heads. We're umpires, not ballboys. Lemur snorts his disgust and starts off at a slow jog in the direction taken by the ball. He'll need to be quicker than that. It's the only ball we've got so if it runs under the wheels of a car, we're scuppered.

While we're waiting for him to get back, Kit appears from the flats with her friend Shelagh. Skooshie's been playing with an empty sherbet dip packet he's found – some wee kid must have thrown it away. He quickly squeezes it back into its original roundness, so it looks full, and holding it out yells, "Hey, Kit – want a sherbet dip?"

He doesn't know what's hit him. She shoves him hard against the wall and hits the sherbet dip packet from his grasp with a vicious backhand swipe.

"**HA! HA! HA!**" she shouts in his face.

Then, after giving me a poke in the shoulder as a parting gesture, she stomps off. Shelagh, who has stood and glared at us throughout the whole episode, gives a dismissive snort and stomps off after her.

"Ow!" says Skooshie, rubbing his shoulder. "Can she not take a joke? I'm hardly likely to give her a real sherbet dip! I'm not made of money!"

"That wasn't why she hit you," says Bru, once he's stopped laughing.

"What did I do?" Skooshie is a picture of wounded innocence.

"You said the words 'sherbet dip'," I say. "You must never – ever – mention them in Kit's presence or she'll think you're looking for a fight."

"Guaranteed," says Bru. "Every time."

"It's only a sherbet dip!"

"Not to Kit. It's a reminder of something embarrassing she did when she was wee. She was about five and my dad gave her 50p to buy me a birthday present. This was in our last house. There was a shop just around the corner and it was the first time she was allowed to go there on her own, so she was really excited. So many things to choose from... She finally decided on a huge, fancy box of chocolates and a sherbet dip."

"And did you enjoy the birthday chocolates, Midge?" asks Bru, who's heard this story before.

"No, I didn't, Bru, thank you for asking. Because Kit ate them! On my birthday she gave me *the sherbet dip* wrapped up as a present."

They find this picture – Kit's chocolate-smeared face and my disappointed one – both outrageous and irresistibly funny. Skooshie nearly chokes with laughter and has to be thumped on the back by Hector.

"Yeah, I know. And when my mum and dad pointed out to her that this wasn't totally fair, that the money was for *my* birthday present, she got all indignant. She said, 'I got him a birthday present. I just bought myself something with the money that was left over!' I'll never let her live it down."

At Lemur's suggestion, we spend the next while looking for Kit. The plan is we'll shout "SHERBET DIP!" at her and run away. Person who doesn't get caught wins. But disappointingly she's nowhere to be found.

"I have never been... so hot... in my entire... life," puffs Hector as we slump down in the shade for a rest. And, like it heard him, the van chooses this moment to put in an appearance, its twinkly tune getting nearer and nearer as it comes up the road.

And the shout goes up, "THE VAN! THE VAN!" Kids drop what they're doing and start sprinting down to where he'll park. Skooshie, Hector and Lemur start fishing in their pockets for money; Bru retrieves his from his sock. We're all flush because there was a wedding at the flats yesterday and we were at the front for the scramble. We had a few skint fingers from it – you have to be quick picking up the money once the bride's dad throws it out the car window.

But my pockets are empty. I've left my money in the house.

"You go down – make sure he doesn't leave before I get there."

My dad says that animals adapt to their environment. "Your platypus," he told me, "is a really clever beast. It's got webbed feet, to help it swim. It's a really good swimmer. It hunts underwater, where it can stay for up to two minutes." (This is longer than Bru or me. We've tried.) (Apparently, it's also a "bottomfeeder" – this turns out NOT to be as funny as you'd think – it just means it eats stuff it finds on the river bottom.) "But it also needs to dig a burrow. Webbed feet not much use for that. So it evolves to a design that means the webbed bit can be pulled back to expose claws."

I still think this is dead cool. I love the idea of giving yourself another power, just because you need it. Like me, living in the high flats. I've got no money and the van comes. I'm a fast runner but that skill's no use to me here. By the time I've run up and down the stairs and down to where the van is parked, it'll've gone – I can guarantee that. The lift I can't rely on – it might be up when I need it down and vice versa. I've used my superhuman brain to solve the problem and given myself the extra power of an extremely loud shout.

I stand under our living-room window and bellow, "MUM! DAD! THE VAN'S HERE!"

I don't have to wait long. The blind shoots up.

"Just a minute... Right, stand back. "

It lands on the ground in front of me with a dull metallic *thud*, 10p in small coins, wrapped in a bit of newspaper. Once again I have successfully avoided being brained. Another instance of boy adapting to his environment. I take the most direct route to the van, which involves jumping over a few walls and leaping down some stairs.

We eat our ice cream leaning against a wall in the last of the sun. In this heat you have to concentrate, licking quickly to catch the drips as they run down the cone. We've all gone for sauce but not flakes – we don't want to use up our money too quickly.

"What flavour is this red stuff supposed to be?" Lemur asks.

"Raspberry," says Hector.

"Oh."

"It's not like the raspberry in raspberry ripple."

"You're right, it's not."

"Or like raspberry jam."

"Yuk. I hate that stuff – it's full of bits that get stuck in your teeth."

"Or like raspberry Angel Delight."

"I've never had that one. Good?"

"Quite nice. Or was it strawberry?"

"None of them are as good as butterscotch."

"Aw, butterscotch! It's magic!"

"Imagine if the van sold butterscotch sauce on ice cream cones!"

We fall silent in admiration. Hector has truly brilliant ideas sometimes.

"Is that Kit?" says Lemur, squinting.

She's holding a cone in one hand and a torch in the other. My torch, to be precise.

"Hey! That's mine, that torch!" But she's too far off to hear and my ice cream is tasting too good for me to get up and chase her.

"She's always taking my stuff," I complain. "You're so lucky to be an only child, Hector."

"Sometimes," says Hector. "A lot of the time it's really boring."

"The annoying thing is," I continue, "that I don't want to use *her* stuff. It's all girly rubbish. Nothing worth taking."

"So you've got to be inventive to get her back?" says Skooshie. Having five brothers and sisters means that Skooshie's experience in this area is impressive. There's not a trick he hasn't used or been the victim of.

"Yeah. I hide things a lot."

"Nice one."

"And tell her she has to do stuff, pretending I'm just passing on the instruction from my mum or dad."

"Yeah, I like that one. There's loads of opportunities for it in my house," Skooshie says. "It's got that you can't really trust what anybody says."

"I can still see her," says Hector, making owl eyes with his fingers to improvise binoculars. "Everybody finished? Could it be Sherbet Dip Time?"

"Yeah!"

And we're off again, in pursuit of Kit. That'll teach her to take my stuff.

12

It's raining: an endless Weegie drizzle that drips and seeps into the den where it finds nooks and crannies we haven't been able to block. We've had days and days of sun, each one hotter than the one before, and the heat has finally exploded in a storm. Today. Friday. Cathkin Day. When we've finally got the jemmy and there's nothing to stop us – except now the weather. We're sitting it out in the den. We're more or less dry, but we're feeling aggrieved, we've nothing to eat and on top of that we're bored. Brain-numbingly bored.

I've just turned to Bru to argue that I'm more bored than he is when Skooshie's bare foot is thrust between our faces.

"Wouldn't it be great," says Skoosh, "if you could hear with your feet?"

"Great how?"

"Well, think about how useful it would be if you were a spy."

"How could that possibly help you in spying on somebody?"

"It would be unexpected. The element of surprise.

People would never suspect you could hear what they were saying."

"Brilliant – except your feet are attached to your legs which are attached to your body which is attached to your head which features your actual ears – which, unless you are very, very, very tall, are within hearing distance of your feet."

"And don't you think people would notice a foot in their face?"

"Aw. You don't think it'll catch on?" says Skooshie. His toes droop, like they're disappointed to hear that.

"Actually, it might work," I say.

"How?"

"Not for eavesdropping. For knocking people out. One whiff and the stink would overwhelm them. Pure dead toxic." Bru and I choke, clutch at our throats and keel over backwards to show how it might go.

Skooshie is delighted.

"Brilliant," he says.

"You can take your foot back now."

This uses up about a minute. Then it's back to being bored.

"Ghost stories!" says Hector, trying to fire us up. "I'll start! Have you heard the one about the headless..."

"... soldier of Battlefield!" we chorus. "Yes, we have!"

"Over and over and over again," I add. It's one of Hector's favourites. We suspect it might be the only ghost story he knows.

"We need some *new* ghost stories," Skooshie sighs.

"I've got one," says Lemur.

"Before you start, Lemur, are you sure (1) that we

haven't heard it before and (2) that it's genuinely scary? Not like that story of Bru's about the thing he thought was under his bed."

"It *was* under my bed and it *was* scary. I was there and I was really scared. It didn't *look* anything like a furry hat."

"No, you said – it looked like an alien."

"Yeah – it was all kind of **WEAHH** and **BLEAHH**." Here Bru gives us a re-enactment of the hat-under-the-bed threat. We've heard this one lots of times before too. Some stories get better when you hear them again. Bru's hat story isn't one of them. It makes you appreciate the headless soldier option, and that's saying something.

"(1) yes and (2) yes," says Lemur. "You haven't heard it before and it is genuinely scary. Do you want to hear it?"

"Go on then." A good job he isn't looking for enthusiasm.

"I'm going to tell you why no one ever has or ever will build on this place where our den is..."

"Wait – can we just fix this? I'm getting soaked."

We help Skooshie tighten up the roof cover. This makes the den a bit less dripped on and also darker.

"Ready? It happened a long, long time ago. There used to be a big house here. A very big house, with a grand staircase – long, curving banisters you could slide down. And there wasn't just one way up to each floor, there were little staircases at the back too: it was a perfect house for Hide and Seek. And there was a huge attic you could explore, full of forgotten junk and lost things and undiscovered treasures.

"The house had grounds too – not just a garden with grass and flowers, but trees and bushes, with hidden tracks and secret places for brilliant dens. Where we're sitting right now – our den – was part of the grounds of the big house."

"How come?" asks Bru, looking round. "There isn't enough space for all that."

"The houses around here didn't exist then," Lemur explains. "No Stanmore Road, no May Terrace. Just this big house. Even Cathkin wasn't built yet. A family called Lorredan lived here and it was called Mount Lorredan House. But twenty years after this story, the house was a ruin... Picture it: completely abandoned and crumbling, with walls you could hardly see under the ivy and brambles. Bats nesting in the bedrooms, cobwebs strung across the broken windows. Everything falling into decay..."

Here he pauses, for a big dramatic effect. Honestly, he's never happier than when he's the centre of attention.

"No one wanted to live in it. Because of what had happened there, they were too scared... In time, the story was forgotten, but people remembered the house and its name survived and became the name for the whole area."

"Mount Lorredan?" says Skooshie. "That's not the name of the area. It's Mount *Florida*, Lemur."

"I do know that, Skooshie," says Lemur.

"But *you* said the area was named after the house." Skoosh doesn't often get to correct Lemur and he's feeling pretty good about this one.

Bru gives him a kick to bring him back down to earth. "Lorredan – Florredan – Florida," he says. "Chinese Whispers kind of thing."

"Aw. Get it."

"It's not *actually* true, anyway – Lemur's just making it up," says Hector. "It's part of the story."

"It *is* in fact true," says Lemur, squaring up for an argument. "Do you *want* to hear the rest?"

I elbow Hector to make him shut up. We don't want Lemur going off in a huff, leaving us without entertainment. Has Hector forgotten how bored we were?

"The man who owned the house was called William Lorredan," Lemur continues. "His family was rich. His grandfather had built a sugar house in the centre of Glasgow..."

"A house actually made of sugar?" Bru cannot believe his ears. "In Glasgow? How come it didn't dissolve in the rain?"

"Not *made of* sugar, Bru – a sugar house was a factory that *made* sugar. They brought the raw sugar on ships from the Caribbean. They refined it in the sugar house – made it pure. They turned it into the sort of white sugar that's used in cakes and sweets."

I can see Bru mentally adding this job to his list of possible future careers.

"The sugar made the family enough money to build Mount Lorredan House, which William inherited when his father died. He wanted to write a book about the Battle of Langside. He'd grown up wandering over the battlefield."

"Splashing through the pools of soldiers' blood on the ground?" says Skooshie, relishing the picture.

"Eh, no... but he did sometimes find souvenirs there, like horseshoes and bits of broken sword. He'd spent all his life trying to imagine how Mary, Queen of Scots felt as she watched her soldiers dying and realised that her only option was to leave her country and flee to England."

Murmurs of sympathy from us at this. Lemur takes the chance to breathe before launching into the next part.

"So, William got married. He and his wife had two sons, Robert and Christy."

"Kirsty? Like Midge's sister? Bit girly."

"Christy, not Kirsty, you eejit. Shush and listen. Ignore him, Lemur. Keep going."

"Robert and Christy loved going with their dad to the site of the battle. It was still just fields then, no houses. 'Listen,' William would say. 'Can you hear the swords clashing? The thundering hooves of the terrified horses? The groans of the men dying in agony?'"

The rain is drumming heavier than before on the roof of the den, not unlike the thundering hooves of terrified horses...

"When Robert was fourteen and Christy twelve, Mr Lorredan had a tree house built in the biggest oak tree in the grounds." Here Lemur pauses significantly. We look at each other. None of us has any idea what an oak tree looks like. He gestures towards the tree Bru and I are leaning against.

"Oh..." We're silently impressed. We've never had a ghost story with actual props before. Lemur is so much better at telling stories than the rest of us. He has us hooked.

"Robert and Christy loved the tree house. They spent a lot of time there. They wanted to think up new games. They were tired of playing at soldiers – it's hard to have a really good battle when there are only two of you. Robert had the idea of playing at pirates."

"Pirates up a tree? Brilliant..."

Lemur ignores Bru's comment and continues.

"At first the tree house was the island where both pirates had hidden their treasure. They were trying to steal the other pirate's loot. They had to defend the island or storm it. But then Christy worked out a way the game could become much more exciting.

"He got a rope. He chose a tree quite close to the tree house, climbed it and crawled out along a thick, high branch. He tied the rope to it. Then he climbed down and tested the knot by hanging onto the rope and jerking it hard. Holding the end of the rope, he climbed back up the tree. Robert watched as his brother swung through the air from one tree to the other, landing in the tree house."

At this Lemur grabs a stick and thrusts it at us, shouting, "**By ancient pirate laws, this ship, the Purple Thistle, belongs to me, Captain Kroniss, and you are defeated, Robber Baron!**"

"Wow!" says Skooshie.

"D'you think *we* could do that?" asks Hector.

"Robert was impressed too," says Lemur, putting the stick down, "and they had a great time playing the pirate game with the rope – until they were caught. Their mother was horrified. Their father laughed and cheered them on. Perhaps he remembered doing things like that when he was young. Perhaps he wanted to be the Robber Baron or Captain Kroniss even now. But when he saw how upset and anxious their mother was, he told them to take the rope down."

"Aw..." A heartfelt groan of disappointment at this turn in events.

"Life was so very, very boring after that. Robert and Christy tried to think up new things to do but they just couldn't forget the pirate game. Then their mother said she was visiting their aunt for a few days. Right away, they had the same idea.

"They stood here holding the rope and looking up at the tree."

Lemur's standing now, gazing upwards. Our eyes are irresistibly drawn upwards too. Unfortunately, our tarpaulin blocks the view of the upper branches, so it feels less awe-inspiring than it should.

"'We could put it back up,' said Christy.

"'We could,' said Robert.

"'What do you think?'

"Robert said nothing.

"'What harm can it do?' said Christy. 'If Mother doesn't know about it, she can't be worried, can she?'

"'That's true,' said Robert. 'We could put it back up just for today.'

"'Or...'

"'Or what?'

"'We could make it more exciting... But maybe you don't dare?'

"'I dare,' snarled Robert. 'Tell me!'"

Sensing that we're getting near the scary part, we all lean forward, anxious not to miss a single word of Lemur's story. And one of us, I'm not blaming anybody but I'm pretty sure it was Hector, catches the overhanging roof tarpaulin with his foot. The rain's been collecting up there for a while. It only takes this slight nudge for the whole roof to cave in, tipping its load of freezing rainwater onto our heads.

13

We struggle to pull the tarpaulin back in place, but there's no chance while it's still raining this hard. We only manage to get even wetter.

"Abandon ship!" yells Bru, and we spill out of the den like a mischief of rats. (That's the actual name for a load of rats – *a mischief*. *A mischief of rats* might be my current favourite. Or maybe *a murder of crows*, I'm not sure. I've remembered a lot of them and I keep trying to drop them into casual conversation. It's a lot harder than you'd think.)

We're standing in Prospecthill Road, wondering what to do next. We're drenched and our hair is plastered to our faces. And it's still pouring with rain.

"It's too wet," says Skooshie. And if even Skooshie thinks that, we're sunk (almost literally). He heads off home down Bolivar Terrace. "I'll see youse later."

He's got a point. The rest of us agree it's time to admit defeat and go home.

"You'll tell us the rest of the story later, Lemur?" I shout through the rain.

"Of course I will," Lemur answers. "Come back when

the rain goes off. I was just getting to the really good bit. See you."

It turns out to be one of those days when the rain just forgets to stop. The sky is a sullen, unchanging grey, just to warn you it can keep piddling down until bedtime. But Bru and I are determined to get back to the den whatever – no way we're going to miss out on the next instalment. So as soon as the downpour slows to a steady drizzle, we risk it.

Lucky we did. When we get to the den, Lemur's there. Somehow he's managed to drag the tarpaulin back in place and it looks like most of the floodwater has soaked away into the ground. Hector and Skooshie turn up a minute later with loads of plastic bags stuffed under their jumpers.

"We thought we could sit on these," says Hector. The settee cushions have absorbed too much water so we spread the bags out on the ground. On the other side of the plastic, the ground shifts soggily beneath our bums. It's not an unpleasant feeling.

"So. Their mum was away and they were thinking of having another go on the swing. But Christy'd had a better idea," Hector summarises and gives Lemur a nod. "On you go, Lemur."

"Christy's idea was this: that they could make a second rope swing on another tree, then race to see who could get to the ship first."

"Pure dead brilliant!" breathes Skooshie.

"Robert thought so too. They picked the second tree carefully. It had to be fair. Robert was a bit taller so he had to start just a bit further away. They climbed their trees. They crawled along branches to tie the ropes. They tested each other's rope by hanging from it.

"Then they took turns swinging to the tree house. It was even better now!

"'It's like flying,' said Robert.

"And then it was back to pirate action.

"'I will recapture the Purple Thistle, you scoundrel,' vowed Robert. 'And then prepare to die when I wreak my terrible vengeance!'

"They stood back to back, like in a duel.

"'**NOW**!'

"They sprinted for their trees – Robert was faster but Christy was a better climber. By the time they had the ropes in their hands, it was impossible to tell who might reach the ship first. Christy leapt, Robert leapt. They swung high across, their feet hitting the tree house platform at exactly the same time. But their legs tangled. Christy only just managed to cling onto his rope. Robert couldn't – he lost his grip and fell. Backwards. Head first. To the ground."

"NO!" All of us at once, thunderstruck.

"He was dead. Their parents were heartbroken, so heartbroken that they forgot all about Christy. Their mother became ill. Christy wasn't allowed to see her. 'Give her time,' his father kept saying. 'She needs time to get over it.' He was so worried about the shock and grief killing his wife, he spent all his time with her.

"No one had any time for Christy.

"Left alone, he wandered about the empty house and grounds. He was strictly forbidden to go into the tree house. He found a knife and carved his own memorial to Robert in the trunk of the tree. He felt cold all the time. And empty. It was like loneliness was eating him away inside.

"Sometimes he would creep quietly up the stairs to his mother's room, in the hope that she might hear his footsteps and call him in. But she never did.

"Christy realised that he was on his own. Robert – he was the only one his parents thought about. He started to wonder if they blamed him for what happened. The rope had been his idea. Robert wouldn't have fallen if they hadn't crashed into each other. It was his fault – all his fault. He couldn't forget how he'd crashed into Robert, their legs tangling – he had laughed, he had thought it was funny. And then watching his brother fall..."

Lemur's voice drops. "He wondered if it would have been better if he had died, not Robert."

Not one of us so much as breathes. We're totally spellbound.

"No one came near the house," Lemur continues. "They were told to stay away because his mother couldn't bear to see anybody. With nothing else to do, with no one paying any attention to him, Christy took advantage of his freedom. There was no one to make him come inside, go to bed, eat properly, be careful. He thought that if he hadn't been alone, it would have been perfect. If only Robert had been there."

Lemur pauses. There's still no ghost, but we're spooked. This isn't the kind of story we were expecting.

"He liked to climb the tree and crouch in the spot where Robert had stood. Of course, they'd cut down the ropes. Cut them down and burned them. He struggled to find another one but it was easy enough to tie it onto the branch once he did.

"He felt a surge of fear as he leapt, then the familiar effortless sensation that was like flying. The first time he landed easily in the tree house. The second time he kicked back off the tree house platform, and swung to and fro until he came to a standstill. He lowered himself to the ground. Then he threw the end of rope up into the tree, so it wasn't hanging down, and went into the house without looking back.

"It was very quiet. No voices. No deep tick-tock from the grandfather clock in the hall. No one had wound it up for weeks. He went up the stairs, looking for his father. He overheard his parents talking in low murmurs in his mother's room. He paused outside to listen. He heard her say, 'But not my Robert, not my Robert...'

"Christy ran out of the house and stumbled across the grass towards the tree. It wasn't because he was crying – he wasn't! – just that he was running so fast. He clambered up the tree in such a hurry he scraped all the skin off his knuckles. He stood up high holding onto the rope. 'This is how you do it, Robert!' he shouted. 'LIKE THIS – LIKE THIS!' And he jumped and he swung towards the tree house. He hit the tree. And dropped onto the ground.

"His father found him later, in the dark, lying on the grass. Christy heard him begging, 'Christy, Christy!', but it was too late. They buried him in the cemetery of the church nearby, beside Robert. Well, at least that's where they took his body... Because somehow, although he was dead, Christy saw it all happening. He saw them carry his coffin out of the house and put it in the carriage. He saw the four black horses with the plumes bobbing on their heads pull the carriage down the drive and away. He saw the coffin lurch as they lowered it into the dark hole in the ground. And he heard the first shovelful of grit hit the lid. The lid of his coffin. He saw his mother crying and he thought that she had left it much too late to be sorry for him.

"Somehow, although he was dead, Christy was still here. Sitting in the tree house, watching without being seen. His parents left the house forever and so it was just him. He waited here for a long time. No one came. The people thought the place was cursed, after what had happened to the boys. Can you imagine being that alone? He felt thin and faded and hollow, like there wasn't enough of him.

"Years passed and the house turned into a ruin. The trees and bushes became overgrown, cutting the house off from the world. By then the story had been forgotten. People sneaked in and took away what they could use. He heard them picking their way through the broken glass and rotten wood, talking and laughing, but he couldn't make them see him. He watched the other houses being built around him, bits of his family's land being stolen. But no one built on this part because he

99

was here. They couldn't see him but they sensed it and they left it alone.

"And he has never left this place. He's still here, still waiting..."

"Aw, magic story, Lemur!"

"Yeah – really exciting."

"Really creepy!"

"Lemur, when you say it happened here – it wasn't that actual tree, was it?"

"That actual tree, Skoosh. The brothers died right there... about where you're sitting. Why do you think it's never been built on?"

Skooshie is open-mouthed. "He's not still here, is he?" he asks.

"Christy? Here in our den?" says Lemur.

"Yes – Christy – the ghost of the boy. Not still waiting here?"

"*Wooooo, Skoooooshie! I'm coming for yoooooo!*" Bru is on him before Skooshie can escape. The rest of us don't hesitate to join in. It's a lot of fun spooking Skoosh and to be honest we're in need of something to relieve the tension.

Skooshie wrestles, pushes us off.

"Does anybody want some chips?" he says. "I'm starving."

14

We don't have any money for chips, so we head for my house. Only my dad's in.

"Where's Mum?"

"She's away into town with Kit."

You hear how Kit is always Kit? I used to be Jamie at home, but since I got into the Grammar, I've been "James". I still look behind me to see who they're talking to. My dad keeps forgetting and so I get the occasional "Jamie" from him, but my mum gives him a Look. So he's taken to saying "James" like he's using quotation marks, which makes it sound a bit sarcastic or like he suspects I'm not who I claim to be. It's disturbing.

We stand, looking hopeful. Skooshie's belly rumbles right on cue.

"Do you lot need feeding?" says my dad, putting his paper down. "We've got some beans and sausages – I could rustle you up a cowboy lunch."

"Aw, thanks, Mr Laird!"

"Your mums know you're here? They'll not be worrying about where you are?"

"She's not in," says Skooshie. "I'd just have to make my own lunch. I'm definitely up for sausages."

"Mine said, 'See you when I see you!'," says Hector.

"And mine'll know that if I'm not at home, I'm here," says Bru.

"Good. What about you, Lemur?"

"Mine won't mind at all," says Lemur.

"Good. Beans and sausages it is! Midge, you sort out some juice."

We sit on the floor in the living room eating our beans and sausages and rolls that my dad's found and buttered. There's too many of us to fit in the kitchen. My dad's in his chair. He says if he sat on the floor, we'd never get him up again.

"Dad," I ask, as we're eating, "d'you know why this area is called Mount Florida?"

"As a matter of fact, I do," says my dad.

My dad's always reading the newspaper and he can talk on any subject under the sun (for a long time). But I've never seen him with an actual book. Even though he's always on at me to study (another example of irony). His allergy to books is a family joke. "Did you find out from a book?" I ask.

"Better than that," he says. "I talked to a man in the pub."

"Had he read a book?" I ask, spearing another sausage.

"Better than that. He was local – his family's lived here for donkey's years. See, that's how you learn things. A book's just one person's point of view. You talk to a lot of people, you get a lot of viewpoints."

"Yeah, Dad. I'll try that one at school. What was he saying, this guy in the pub?"

"He said there used to be a big house here – a long time ago, before Cathkin, before Hampden, before any of the houses that are here now were built. Mount Florida was named after the house."

Lemur shoots Hector a triumphant look.

"He remembered his dad showing him a map of the area with the house marked on it as a ruin."

"Lemur," I say, "can we tell my dad your story?"

We all chip in, so it loses a lot of its dramatic effect but we're too excited to let Lemur tell it on his own. We keep the details vague so we don't give away the location of our den. My dad doesn't ask awkward questions.

"Aw, that's a good story," he says when we've finished. "Did you think it all up yourself, Lemur?"

"It's actually true, Mr Laird."

"Is that right?" says my dad.

"So who told you it?" asks Hector.

"It's a family story," says Lemur.

"It's great how stories get passed on," says my dad. "Right, are you all finished?"

"Thanks for that, Mr Laird," says Skooshie, licking the last of the bean sauce off his plate. "You're a great cook!" He actually means it.

"Yeah, Dad," I say. "Nobody can heat up beans quite like you."

"Well, they don't call me Gordon Blue for nothing," says my dad. "Are you done licking, Skooshie? You maybe better stop before you take the pattern off the plate."

He collects up all the plates and takes them into the kitchen. He brings back the biscuit tin with him.

"Now, here's what I'm wondering," he says. "D'you think Christy did it on purpose? Made himself fall from the tree?"

Hector thinks yes: it's too much of a coincidence. Bru and Skooshie think definitely not: from what they've heard about Christy, they don't see him as the type to give up that easily.

"I think it might be more complicated than that," I say. "I mean, I don't think he wanted to kill himself but I think he knew he was taking a big risk. Maybe he thought it was worth it."

"That's what I think," says Lemur. "That he loved doing it too much to give it up."

"And you say his ghost's still in the den?" says my dad.

"Well, Lemur's saying that," says Skooshie. "I don't see how it can be true."

"Really, Skoosh?" says Bru. "You've never noticed that funny noise – the branches above us creaking like there's somebody up there, sitting and watching us?"

My dad laughs as Skooshie tightens his hand into a fist and makes a silent gesture to Bru that means "Just you wait till we get outside..."

"Well," Dad says, "if he is there, I don't think you've got anything to worry about. As ghosts go, he sounds exactly your type: clever, loyal, adventurous. He'll fit in perfectly."

We're back in the den. For once, things are quiet, maybe too quiet... It's because of the Wagon Wheels that we picked up at Hector's on the way here. Wagon Wheels present a particular biscuit-eating challenge, if you're determined to enjoy them in the time-honoured traditional way. That involves dealing with the top layer first to expose the creamy, marshmallowy centre, which is at its most delicious if you eat it in its pure state. With, say, a Bourbon or a Jammie Dodger it's pretty straightforward, because you can get a good grip on the bottom. Not so with Wagon Wheels. It's definitely a huge part of their attraction that they're totally covered in chocolate, but it makes the task trickier. You need to start by creating a handhold. I like to go all the way round the circumference – some people lick the edge clean of chocolate, but I prefer the nibbling approach. It's more satisfying. Once that's done, that's when I start licking. It's the best way to eat the chocolate covering the top layer. Then you prise the biscuit off in big crunchy bites. Now for the marshmallow. It collects in sweet, claggy lumps in your mouth as you drag your teeth across the surface. Fantastic... In a perfect world you'd be able to eat everything but the filling, leaving it to the very last. But it's not humanly possible. Yet.

"Did you know," says Hector, simultaneously swallowing his last mouthful of Wagon Wheel, "that there's no word in Gaelic for yes?" His biscuit-eating technique clearly needs work: he's always finished ages before anybody else.

"So how do you answer the question 'Do you want a Wagon Wheel?'"

"I don't think they have Wagon Wheels in the wilds up north," says Skooshie, munching thoughtfully.

"Did *you* know," says Bru, "that there's no word in any language for that smell Hector just produced?"

"That'll be the beans..."

" **AAAAAH!** It's getting worse."

"EVACUATE! EVACUATE!"

Kit's sitting up in her bed in the dark, cross-legged like a pixie. She's desperate to know what happens. So desperate that she doesn't say anything at all until I've got to the very end. (That's a first.)

"So why did Christy stay and Robert didn't?" she asks then.

"Good question," I say. "Why's he restless? Maybe he feels guilty about Robert dying?"

"And he's doomed to roam the earth in punishment?"

"Wouldn't there be more howling and rattling of chains if that was true?" I ask. We watched *A Christmas Carol* on telly last year, so I'm something of an expert on restless ghosts.

"D'you think the story's true, Midge?" Kit asks.

"Yeah."

"*Really?*"

My first instinct is to go for it, to play up the scariness of our haunted den, because it's always fun to frighten Kit. But in my heart I know she's not as gullible as Skoosh.

"It might have actually happened, I suppose," I say.

"It's a great story and I want it to be true. But I don't really think there's a ghost in our den. And I'm pretty sure Bru and Hector think the same way. Skooshie – well, he's practically weeing himself with fear, so I guess he believes it!" Kit giggles. "Lemur's enjoying winding Skooshie up so much – he's saying it's all completely true and that the ghost is right there... '*Ooooh, Skooshie, mind out behind you!*' I don't think he's had this much fun in ages!"

"Poor Skooshie!"

"Ha! Like you won't mention it next time you see him!"

More giggles. "Well, I might. So Lemur's a good storyteller?"

"Yeah – loads of drama and tension. And pure dead brilliant details – my favourite is the bit about Christy watching his own coffin being lowered into the ground..."

"Spooky... and weird. Though Lemur is, isn't he? Weird, I mean."

"You always say that. It's just because he lives in a big house."

"No, I don't mean that. It's all the stuff you don't know about him."

"Like what?"

"Well, what school is he going to at the end of the summer?"

"I'm not sure."

"What primary school did he go to? He wasn't at ours."

"I'm not sure."

"Well, what colour was his uniform?"

I have no picture in my head of Lemur in his school uniform. He must always have changed out of it. Or did I just not notice? Does anybody notice that kind of thing, apart from girls?

"I'm not sure. This is what you're basing your accusation of weirdness on – that we don't know what colour his school tie is?"

"Did you never ask? You spend your entire time together! What do boys actually talk about?"

"*Loads* of different stuff. Big, *important* stuff! Not school."

She sighs and lies down. "Maybe it's just boys in general that are weird."

The truth is I've avoided asking Lemur about school. I would definitely feel less worried about secondary if Lemur was going to be there. But to find that out, we'd need to discuss it and that's the last thing I want to do. School's something we've all agreed – without ever mentioning the subject at all – not to talk about. As far as I know, I'm the only one going to the Grammar. So I'll be cutting past Cathkin on my own every morning. And Bru, Skooshie and Hector will be getting the bus in the opposite direction without me. Lemur never talks about school – he says it's irrelevant. (He told Skooshie that wasn't the actual name of his school. Skooshie punched him.)

So we don't talk about what will happen in August. I know I'm abandoning them all and I really don't deserve to have Lemur coming with me. It wouldn't be fair. Thing is, if I don't ask and Lemur *is* there, then I haven't caused that – that's just chance. So then that would be OK. I think.

15

It's the next day and it's still raining. Kit and I stare out the window but watching the rain and willing it to stop doesn't seem to be working. We entertain ourselves for a while by breathing on the cold glass to fog it up and using our fingernails to draw mist pictures. My best one shows Kit looking like a pig. She adds a speech bubble to it that says OINK!, so I think she quite likes it. Then we're spotted and told off and all our artwork is erased in one sweep of a window cloth. We retreat to our bedroom with nothing to do. What is it about wet weather that clears all the good ideas out of your brain?

"Tell me a story," Kit says.

"I don't know any." That's not of course true. I just haven't got the oomph.

"Tell me Lemur's story," she insists.

"I've told you that already. Loads of times."

"Twice!" she protests. "I really like it. That's why I want to hear it again. You're good at the bit where he's *falling, falling, falling – CRASH! Dead!*"

"I am quite good at that bit," I admit. But I'm not flattered enough to tell the story for the 932nd time.

"I wonder if Lemur knew the story and went looking for the place to make his den? Or whether he made his den first and then made up the story to go with it?"

"It is not *Lemur's* den – it's *our* den! In fact, *I* found it, so if it's anybody's, it's mine. Well, actually, Bru's and mine – we found it together."

"Really? I always thought it was Lemur's first, because he and it turned up about the same time."

"You're right, they did," I say. "I found them both on the same day – well, I met Lemur, and then I – I mean we – found the den."

"What happened?"

"We were playing at spies – Bru, Hector, Skooshie and me. They were trying to hunt me down. I had concealed about my person some incredibly **TOP-SECRET** plans – plans to do with... Well, if I told you, I'd have to kill you. Let's just say the safety of Scotland depended on me not getting caught and you're better off not knowing." I've got this far before I realise Kit's managed to trick me into telling her a story. Annoying, but by now it's too late, so I keep going.

"So, I was bombing it down May Terrace, looking over my shoulder to see if they were on my tail and – **THUMP!** Straight into something hard. Next thing I knew I was on the ground and so was this other boy. Totally my fault. He was rubbing his shoulder and – surprisingly – not looking too annoyed.

"'I'm really sorry,' I said, helping him up. 'It's just I'm on the run.'

"'I know – I saw them earlier. They're not far from here.'

"'Is there anywhere I can hide?'

"'Quick, in here!' We ducked behind a bush by the side of a house. 'Breathe more quietly!' he said. 'They'll hear you!' We stood in complete silence, me holding my breath until I was ready to burst. Hector, Skooshie and Bru came panting up the road, stopped right in front of the bush and looked round in all directions.

"'No sign of him,' said Bru. 'Aw, I think we've lost him.'

"'OK,' said Hector. 'Back to base.'

"They cleared off. I couldn't believe my luck. 'That means I've won! I better go and tell them how hopeless they are. Thanks for giving me somewhere to hide – it was brilliant.' As the boy turned to go back down May Terrace, I had a better idea. 'If you've nothing else to do,' I said, 'you could come and hang about with us?'

"And the boy-who-wasn't-yet-Lemur grinned and said, 'OK.'

"Hector, Skooshie and Bru wouldn't believe they'd been two feet away from me and hadn't caught me.

"'Not possible!' said Skooshie. 'We're too highly trained.'

"'Show them,' said Lemur. And so we went back to May Terrace and showed them the bush. They took turns to investigate and admit I was right.

"'Hey,' said Bru from behind the bush. 'It goes deeper, you know.'

"We slipped in after him, one by one. We fought our way along the path, pushing away the leaves and branches that sprang back in our faces. It was a tight fit with us all and there was some shoving – and the next thing you know I'd fallen through the undergrowth into the space that was to become our den."

"Oh," says Kit when I've finished.

"Oh what?"

"Just funny they both happened at the same time. Meeting Lemur and finding the den."

"I know! It is *very* rare that two brilliant things happen in one day."

"Unless it wasn't an accident."

"What are you on about?"

"Maybe Lemur got in your way on purpose when you were running? Maybe he meant you to find the den and just made it look like you were the one to discover it?"

"Why would he do that?"

She doesn't get a chance to answer because the door goes. It's Bru, which is what I call timely. He bounces himself into a comfortable position on my bed and listens as I bring him up to speed on what Kit and I have been talking about. Bru chips in with extra details of the den discovery. "Great day," he says, when we've finished.

"Yeah. The best. And she thinks Lemur set it up." I snort and flick my eyes dismissively in Kit's direction.

"You're saying it wasn't just chance, Kit?" says Bru. "Lemur arranged it so Midge'd bump into him and that we'd find the den?"

"Yes. I am."

"Well... maybe he did. And if he did, it all worked out. Maybe he saw us playing and he was lonely and he thought the quickest way to get to meet us was to let himself be knocked over like a bowling pin by you, Midge."

"I did hit him hard!"

"And maybe he thought the best way for us to be

friends was to have something in common, like the den. And he didn't want to say, 'Here's my den and you can hang out here with me,' because then it would always have been *his* den."

"Yes. Much better for it to be something that we all discovered at the same time, so it was always *ours*, for all of us. So you think he probably did set it up?"

Bru shrugs. "I don't know for sure. But it's totally Lemur, isn't it?"

"Clever... always wanting to be totally in charge... generous... scheming..."

"Yeah. All of these. That's just Lemur."

He's right. Bru's usually right. It's annoying he thinks Kit was right too, but sometimes you just have to accept these things.

The next thing we hear is a whine from her: "Will you play a game with me? Pullleeeeease?"

There's a bit of argument about what to play. Kit says we can't play Mouse Trap because the bath is missing. I say that if it is, she's the one who lost it. She says I can't prove that. I say... but Bru interrupts, suggesting a Connect 4 league. Kit and I both say no to that – one person would have to sit out every game, which would be boring. We're about to settle for playing cards when Kit remembers Go.

Go's a bit like Monopoly, but much more interesting – you get to travel round the world collecting souvenirs. You choose where you want to go. You need to change your money to the currency of every place you land in so you can buy them. The first one back to London with all their souvenirs is the winner.

"Mum's not doing anything – just drinking tea and reading a magazine. Shall we ask her if she wants to play as well?" says Kit. She comes back two minutes later without Mum but with a tray of biscuits and juice. "She says she's sorry, she's busy, but she hopes we enjoy playing."

"I love this game," says Bru, just before a Risk card sends him to Heard Island when he was on his way to Los Angeles. He curses as he looks at his now-useless US dollars. "How is it even possible to be diverted from the US to some squitchy wee island near Australia? What kind of storm causes that?"

Kit looks gleeful. She has a fistful of souvenirs and I can see her working out what's the quickest route back to London. She looks on target to win. I need to distract her.

I pick up her souvenirs.

"What are you doing?" she says. "Buy your own."

"Just wanted to see which ones you've gone for. Oh, yeah. Here you are."

"What do you mean, 'Oh, yeah'?" she asks, snatching them back.

"Nothing."

She rolls the dice and moves. She can't let it go. "You definitely meant something."

"Just that they're not like the souvenirs you normally go for."

"How?"

"You usually have quite an ambitious route, don't you? The way you're going is a bit... easy?" I catch Bru's eye. He knows exactly what I am up to. "But you're absolutely right. It's winning that's important," I say, taking my turn with the dice. "Not winning in style."

You can almost hear the cogs turning in Kit's tiny brain as she takes this in. She can see that if she wins using her current plan, I am going to go on and on about this. That it was a win but somehow not a very impressive one. But if she changes her plan and then loses, she will have played right into my hands. Her only option is to change her plan and still make sure she wins.

With her next move she goes so far west she is off the board. She throws her piece to Bru. "Tokyo," she says. He places it for her. I have to conceal a smile. It's a long way from Tokyo to London...

I study the board. I'm plotting a very bold route myself, involving all three African locations. And it's going really well. Up until the point when Bru rolls a six and hops his piece casually across the Atlantic. "That's me," he says. "Back in London."

"Never mind," he adds, grinning at how crushed we look. "You both lost with a lot of style."

The rain clears at last after dinner. Kids ooze out of the flats and try to find games that don't involve going on the grass, which is still soaking wet. The air is thick and sticky.

We're playing Kick the Can. It's never hard to find a Tennants can – the fans on their way to Hampden sling them into the long grass as they go up the hill.

Kick the Can is like Hide and Seek, but more exciting. You stand an empty can in the place where whoever's het is counting. When he goes to look for everybody, you have to try and get back to base and kick the can over – it's proof you made it back safely. If he sees you and is able to kick the can over first, you're out.

It's Skooshie's turn to be het.

Bru's really good at this game. He's small and fast and really hard to spot. He's the first back as usual. Skooshie's miles off when Bru gives the can a mighty punt, so it ricochets off the wall. "HOME!" he yells.

I manage to steal in. I'd like to say it's because I'm a faster runner than Skooshie but I was helped a bit by Bru showing Skooshie a really interesting stone he'd just found. "NO FAIR!" shouts Skooshie.

"All's fair in war and Kick the Can!" I correct him. "HOME!" Again the can batters off the wall.

By now Skooshie can hardly see. The lights start to go on in people's windows, making the gloaming even darker. While Skooshie's complaining that this gives all the hiders a huge advantage, a flash of sandshoes gives Hector away. Skooshie races for the can, beating Hector back.

"Saw your shoes," says Skooshie, doubled-over and breathless. "Wear your dark ones next time."

"These ones are the best for running," says Hector, also gasping.

Only Lemur hasn't been found.

We don't think about being called in, in case thinking about it will make it happen. We would give anything to stay out, anything.

The door to my flats opens. A figure stands looking out at us. I squint at it, trying to work out who it is. It's not my dad because I know he's not working tonight. And the figure doesn't move towards us, just stands, peering into the dark. I wonder if we're in for a row. Not everybody appreciates hearing a good game of Kick the Can.

"James!" It's a man, beckoning to me. I jog over. As I get closer, I recognise Mr Murphy. His windows are all on the other side of the flats. No way he could hear us playing.

"Hello, Mr Murphy."

"Is your pal with you?"

"Which pal?"

"The lad with the fair hair who was with you... that other day at the lift. What do you call him?"

"Lemur?" I say.

"Lemur," he repeats thoughtfully. "Is he here?"

"He's not here right now. We're playing a game and he's hiding. I've no idea where he is."

"Does he live in the flats?"

"No."

"Tell him... Will you ask him to come and see me? Tell him I said it's about time we had a talk."

"OK, Mr Murphy. I will."

"Thanks."

He turns to go. I really want to ask him what it's about but I'm not sure how to do it without getting told off for nosiness.

"Is it... is it anything important, Mr Murphy?" I finally ask, in what I hope is a casual kind of way.

He looks at me. Here's the row coming.

"Good pal of yours?" he asks.

I nod. "Yeah, he is."

"Watch out for him. Just watch out for him."

Watch out for Lemur? Why? I have no time to ask. Mr Murphy is gone, back in the lift on the way up to his flat.

Is Lemur in trouble, like Kit said? What has he done? What do I need to do to help him? I lie in bed later, thinking and thinking, but I don't come up with any answers.

I get Lemur on his own the next day and I pass on the message.

"Are you in trouble, Lemur? Because if you are..."

"I'm not in trouble."

"What did he mean then?"

"He saw us playing?"

"Yeah."

"Probably remembering when he was in a gang. Remembering what it's like to have your pals round you, standing up for you. Just saying we should watch out for each other, whatever happens."

"We do. That's what I was going to say. If you are in trouble—"

"Which I'm not."

"I know you're not. But if you ever are... well... you know... I'm... if you need... you know... help."

"Eh, yeah. OK."

I know – it's starting to sound like the kind of conversation two girls might have. I think we're both relieved when Skooshie tumbles into the den, throwing out noisy accusations that Lemur cheated with his hiding place the night before, and normality is restored.

16

"I can't, Midge." Bru's just answered the door to me. There's a resigned look on his face. "My mum's going out and I've got to look after the Toaty Terrors."

"An-drew!"

"Sorry, got to go. See you later maybe?"

"I'll help."

"Really? Would you? No, but don't. They're a pain. That would be above and beyond, you know."

"I'm not going to abandon you."

"Aw, thanks, Midge. You're a pal."

Mrs Brown gives me a smile when I go into Bru's living room.

"*Two* big brothers to play with. You're brave, Jamie!"

Bru's five-year-old twin brothers, Kenny and Graham – more usually known as the Toaty Terrors – fling themselves at me. "Midge! What're we going to do? What're we going to play? What're we going to do?"

"Enjoy yourselves!" Mrs Brown calls after us. They're still attached to me as we leave the house and get in the lift.

"How hard can it be?" I ask Bru, as the lift doors open and his brothers whirl out (and when I say "whirl", I mean whirl – all the way down they've been spinning to see who can make themselves the dizziest). "As long as we don't lose them... Or let them injure themselves... And they don't start crying... That about covers it, doesn't it? See. We'll be fine. Then as soon as we get rid of them, it's up to the den to make the final arrangements for Friday."

Bru says nothing. It's possible that he's thinking that I don't know what I'm talking about, but if he is, he's not the sort to say it.

"Do that spinning thing again," he calls to Kenny and Graham. "Here on the grass, where it won't hurt when you fall down."

We sit and watch, admiring them, for a minute.

"You'd fall down before me," says Bru.

"Prove it," I answer.

"You're on." Bru never says no to a challenge.

Bru is the first to drop. As I knew he would be. Kenny and Graham shout gleefully for another round, all of us together. We let them win, or maybe you get less good at this sort of thing as you get older. The four of us lie whooping on the grass. I keep my eyes closed to enjoy the last moments of the wheeling, out-of-control feeling you get.

"What're we doing now?" asks Kenny.

We try to teach them how to play tennis. It's a dead loss. They don't seem to get the whole ball-racquet connection thing. If Bru and I aren't ducking to avoid head injury from the wildly swung racquets, we're sprinting down the hill after the ball. We all agree it's time to find another activity.

We go up to play on the bars. I think they're supposed to be for people to hold onto as they go up and down the stairs but we all use them for tricks. We show the TTs how to turn somersaults, then hold onto them as they have a go, to make sure they don't split their heads open on the concrete. They get quite good.

"Monkey genes," says Bru.

"That makes sense," I say. "How long have we done so far?"

"Half an hour," says Bru.

"You're kidding!"

He shakes his head. "They actually make time go slower. Didn't you know? I think it's their superpower."

"What're we doing now?" asks Graham, who's hanging upside down. If he didn't have the ginger hair, he'd look quite like a vampire bat.

"What about a game of Spies?" I suggest.

"I'm James Bond," Kenny announces quickly.

"No, I'm James Bond!" says Graham, now the right way up and looking less batty. "I'm dead good at being a spy!"

"No – me." Kenny gives his brother a push. Graham gives him a push back. These things never stop at one push each. It's not looking promising.

"Whoa!" says Bru. "Why d'you want to be James Bond? The Russian spies are much more dangerous."

"Russians?" says Graham, suspiciously. "Who are *they*?"

"They're... from Russia. They've got bombs. We've got bombs. They spy on us all the time and we spy on them. That's the main spying thing that's actually going on right now in the world at this very minute. The Russians practise a lot and are really good at spying – they've got lots of amazing gadgets. You should definitely be Russians."

"So, these Russians, they beat James Bond?"

"Well, no..."

"They sound rubbish," says Kenny.

"Yeah," says Graham.

"Let's both be James Bond, Graham," says Kenny.

"Yeah!" says Graham.

The flats are a great place for spying (well, if you can forget the fact that you can be seen from about a million different windows). There's loads of walls to hide behind, lots of different ways you can go to avoid capture, plenty of places to hide. We give Kenny and Graham a head start by talking loudly in Russian accents whenever we're getting close to them, to warn them we're on their trail. Bru and I agree our accents are brilliant, even if totally unappreciated by Kenny and Graham. It turns out we don't know any real Russians apart from Olga Korbut (and she's a girl), so we go by the code names Midgeski and Bruski.

Using all our cunning, and some very skilful Russian spy tactics, we eventually capture the Jameses Bonds and are just about to make sure that they never cause us any trouble again, when, totally unexpectedly... they manage to escape! (Who could have guessed that was going to happen?) As they run off, the Jameses Bonds pause only to shoot the brilliant Russian agents Bruski and Midgeski, who die slowly, dramatically, tragically...

"Aren't you *dead* yet?" says Graham.

"What're we doing now?" asks Kenny.

It's quite hard work, thinking up all these great things to do.

"What would you like to do? What ideas have you two got?" I ask them hopefully.

Kenny frowns. "We don't have any ideas."

"That's *your* job," Graham adds. There's a hint of a warning in his voice. Bru wasn't kidding. They are tough customers.

The van comes. Bru's mum has given us money. Going down to the van (the long way), queuing (politely allowing grannies to go before us) and eating our ice creams uses up another ten minutes.

"What're we doing now?" asks Graham.

Bru and I have noticed that there are quite a few other wee kids at the van. We try to interest Kenny and Graham in playing with their own kind, but they're not having it. Even when one of the wee kids comes up and asks if he can play.

"No," says Graham. "We're playing a game with my big brother."

"That's who I meant," says the wee kid. "It's him I want to play with."

It is risky but we're stuck for ideas so we don't have a lot of choice. We started off with two and now there's a whole crowd of them wanting entertainment from us. Luckily, Bru comes up with a brilliant plan.

"OK, you can all play. D'you know Hospital Tig?"

They don't. When we explain it, they look at us like we're aliens, bringing details of an amazing new technology from another planet. Even Kenny and Graham seem impressed.

"Right, listen!" says Bru. "Rule 1. One person is het. They do the chasing. Everybody else runs. You have three lives. If you're caught, you lose a life. First person to lose all three lives is then het."

"Rule 2 – and this is why it's called Hospital Tig. If the person who's het catches you by touching you on the arm, after that you've got to run holding your arm. If you're caught on the head, you hold your head. Get the idea?"

There's a chorus of yeses, and more than one "Yes, Kenny and Graham's big brother."

"Rule 3. You can only run in this big space between the flats – the stairs are too dangerous, so they're out of bounds. We don't want any actual hospitals involved, do we?" As jokes go, it's really pathetic – if we hadn't had the audience, I would have had to punch Bru to bring him to his senses. But the wee kids laugh like he's the funniest person they've ever met.

I'm het first. There's a lot of shrieking and squealing as they scarper. I do give them a chance by running sideways a lot of the time. My target (one that I've just made up for myself) is to catch them all in different ways to see who runs the funniest. I get a wee fair-haired girl by touching her hair as it flies out behind her when she sprints, so she has to run holding her plait up in the air. Then I duck right down and manage a neat backhand tap to Graham's ankle. (Not easy – being so toaty, he's really very near the ground.) After that, he's got to hop so he can hold onto it. And I flick Kenny on both buttocks, so he has to run around holding his bum. This has most of the wee folk in stitches (now *that*, Bru, is what *I* call a genuinely funny hospital joke). This makes it a lot easier to catch them.

We play until Bru and I are exhausted.

"How come little kids are so hard to tire out?" I say. We're sitting on the steps at the edge of the grass, watching them run away from each other, clutching their heads, their legs, their backs. It's the funniest thing I've seen in a while.

"Don't know. It might be because they sleep a lot. Or maybe just all the sugar."

"Hey – that's cheating! You're not allowed on the steps. You said!" They are onto us.

"That's right. Well done for noticing that. The reason we're here is because that's the game finished now."

There's a howl of protest.

"No, that's it. That was good and thanks very much for playing."

"Yeah, excellent running. Never seen so many fantastic players of Hospital Tig. OK – now go and... play your other games."

The grumble of disappointment takes a while to die away – and I hear in the midst of it at least one ungrateful "Spoilsports!" – but they do drift off and in a few minutes are busy doing whatever it was they were doing before the Bru & Midge Show came into town. Only Kenny and Graham remain, panting, red cheeked and crazy haired.

"What're we doing now?" asks Kenny.

"Well..." Bru turns away from them, pretending to scan the surroundings in search of new fun activities. "What's the time?" he mutters to me. "Don't make it obvious."

I yawn and stretch, using this crafty ploy to glance at my watch. "Nearly half seven."

"At last. Hey – Kenny, Graham. We're really thirsty after all that running around. What about you? We were thinking we'd just go up and get a drink."

Kenny eyes him suspiciously. "And then we're coming back out?"

"Well, it's not even dark yet!" says Bru, like he's surprised by Kenny's question.

"What're we doing when we come back out?"

"Need to think about that. C'mon."

The Toaty Terrors entertain themselves in the lift on the way up by seeing how many times they can jump on our feet. Toaty they might be, but it's a lot like sharing the lift with a herd of dancing baby elephants.

Bru directs them out of the lift and into the house with the patience of a man who's about to be reprieved.

"Hi, Mum. I think you said we should come up and Get A Drink at half seven," says Bru meaningfully. "It's half seven now."

"Okey dokey," says Bru's mum. "You must be thirsty after all that playing. Was it fun? You'll have to tell me all about it. Now... oh, wait a minute. I don't know if I've got any juice. Kenny, can you look in that cupboard and see if there's any there? Or there might be some behind the kitchen door – Graham, you have a look there." Out of the twins' eyeshot, she waves her hand at us to go. We sneak out backwards.

But they're not as easy to fool as you'd think because as we're creeping up the hall, we hear a wail, "Bru! Bru! You said we were going back out!"

We make a run for it.

17

I spot Lemur coming down the hill, through the long grass. I'm pleased to see him. He was here yesterday – he's a regular for Wednesday morning viewings of *The Flashing Blade* now, but apart from that it's been a long while since he came for me. We'd arranged to meet at the den this morning but he must want to say something about getting into Cathkin tomorrow before the others get there. (We're so close – it's definitely going to happen tomorrow – definitely!) . It's really early but I'm just about dressed. The window's open the small amount the safety catch allows. I'm about to shout down to him and wave, then I have a better idea.

I wait by the side of the lift. My plan is I'll leap out as soon as the door opens, and scare the life out of him. I watch the numbers in the bar above the door light up in turn, so I can time it right. It always takes ages to get to 6, which gives me time to plan. 1, 2... I'm thinking King Kong style, full roar. 3, 4... I'm wishing I'd brought something I could use as a sword – more dramatic, scarier. 5... No time for other ideas, King Kong it is. 6...

7?

I get it.

He saw me at the window. He worked out what I was going to do and now he's going to leap down the stairs and get *me* as I cross the stairs landing back to my house. No chance. I'm ready for him. I open the door to the stairs slowly, crouching down to make myself less of a target. On the next floor up I hear the door from the lift to the stairs open, hear it swing shut. I don't breathe. I'm ready to pounce. Footsteps cross the space between the fire doors on the stair landing. The second door swings shut. He's waiting to make sure I've fallen for it. But then I hear a third door, the one that takes you into the space outside flats 74 and 75. He's standing outside Mr Murphy's house.

What is he playing at? My mum will give me hell if we end up annoying Mr Murphy. The game's a bogey. I need to get him out of there. I go up the stairs to floor 7 and through the fire door, making as little noise as possible. As long as Mr Murphy doesn't open his door and catch us messing about, we're OK.

Lemur's not there.

I can't see him outside Mr Murphy's. And he's not hiding behind the rubbish chute. I go all the way round floor 7, past the lift – which is still on this floor. I go back out to the stair landing by the other fire door. He's nowhere. And I realise I will find him outside my house, looking smug and ready to crow about how easily he tricked me.

But he's not there either.

I go back in. "Has Lemur been here?" I ask Kit, who's lying on a sunny patch of carpet in the living room, colouring in.

"No," says Kit.

"Sure?" I ask, looking at her hard.

"Yeah, I'm sure. He's quite hard to miss."

"He didn't tell you to say that?"

"Midge, he hasn't been here. Why do you think he has?"

"Never mind." I don't tell her, because she'd find it funny that my plan backfired.

So I just wait for Lemur to appear. I wait for him to get bored with keeping me waiting. I wait, very bored, for a long time and he still doesn't turn up. Kit keeps colouring in for a while, then Shelagh turns up and they go out.

I hear somebody yelling my name from outside. It's Hector – he's standing down on the road, at the bottom of the hill. He's been running.

"Hey," I shout back.

"*C'mon!* Where've you been?"

"Here – waiting for Lemur."

He looks confused. "Lemur's with the others, at the den. We said we'd meet there. We're all waiting for *you.*"

Kit and Shelagh are playing on the bars halfway up the hill. Kit is practising pulling herself up backwards to grip on to the bar with her legs, then reaching down to flick off in a handstand. She's getting quite good at it.

"No Lemur?" she shouts as we trudge through the long grass up the hill.

I ignore her.

When we get to the den, Lemur's in full flood: "The defender tackles, knocks the ball clear to the side, then punts it up into the air – *HIGH, HIGH, HIGH!* the crowd shout – that's how the team got their nickname, you know, the Hi Hi's – Anderson runs back to collect it, then there's a blur of red as he sprints down the wing. He's unstoppable! *GOALLLLL!* Oh, there you are... You're really late, Midge."

"I saw you coming down the hill. I was waiting for you – I thought you were coming to get me."

He gives a laugh of surprise. "I didn't say I was coming to your house today, did I? Didn't we agree to meet here?"

"I know. But then I saw you and I thought it was a change of plan."

"It wasn't that other boy, Midge?" Skooshie chips in helpfully.

We all turn and look at him, bemused.

"*What* other boy?"

"The one who looks like Lemur. The one that Mr Murphy confused Lemur with. It's funny we've never seen him before."

"Shut up, Skoosh. It was Lemur I saw."

"The plan was to meet here." Lemur speaks slowly and deliberately, like he thinks I'm a bit dim and I need help understanding. "And here I am. And here you are... At last."

"You must have been seeing things, Midge." Hector grins. "Or you need glasses. It'll be all that studying you've been doing."

"Shut up, Hector," I growl. "I didn't imagine it. Lemur's lying."

"I never lie!"

We're standing right in the middle of the den – Lemur and me, eye to eye – much too close to each other for this not to turn into a fight.

"Aw, don't argue," says Bru, pushing us away from each other. "C'mon. Lemur's been telling us about Third Lanark, the team that used to play at Cathkin. We were imagining what they were like, back in their heyday."

"And what Cathkin must have been like with the stands full. A pity your flats weren't built then, Midge. You'd've had a brilliant view!"

"Yeah," says Hector. "We'd all've got to watch for nothing!"

I find that a cheering idea. I nudge Hector with my foot – well, it's more of a kick. It makes me feel better. "Move over. You're taking up all the room. So, how come you know so much about this team? Did you ever see them?"

"He couldn't've. The stadium shut down about ten years ago, my dad says. They went bankrupt," says Bru. "When you think about it, they couldn't've been that good if nobody wanted to see them."

"My dad says that the year I was born, they lost 30 matches out of 34. That's not good."

"They *were* good," says Lemur. "Not at the end but before. They were one of the first teams in the Scottish League, right back in the 1880s. They won it 1904 and the Scottish Cup in 1889 and 1905. They used to be better than Rangers and Celtic.

"Their strips were red because at first the team was

made up of soldiers – the Third Lanarkshire Rifles. Their uniform was red. That's where the name's from – Third Lanark."

How does he know all this stuff? Not for the first time, I wonder how much of it he invents. He's got a vivid imagination, as my mum would say – and obviously that's something you want in a friend. But the others, they know – and I know – when they're making stuff up. Does Lemur? He says he doesn't lie but I'm not sure he's always clear on the boundaries between real life and fantasy.

But it's hard to stay very annoyed with him. His stories are entertaining even if they're not totally true. Plus we need to be a team if we're going to get into Cathkin. It's really going to happen. Tomorrow we're actually going to be there. For definite this time.

"Bye, Midge!" shouts Skooshie, as we split up to walk home. "Don't forget to ask your mum to take you for that eye check-up!" He disappears down Bolivar Terrace, snorting with laughter. I want to throw a rock at his head.

And then I turn round to find that Kit's waiting on the other side of Prospecthill Road. She's strictly forbidden to cross it on her own. That road is our moat, the wall around our Troy. If we stay on this side of it, Kit can't get to us.

"You've to hurry up," she calls across. "Mum says it's dinnertime."

She's so annoying. This was my one chance to talk to Bru. It has been completely impossible to get him on his own to tell him about Mr Murphy saying I should watch out for Lemur – if it's not wee brothers, it's the rest of them getting in the way – and now here's Kit joining in! And I know he won't take sides in the argument Lemur and I have just had, but I need to tell him I *did not* imagine it. I say nothing, Bru says nothing, Kit says nothing, all the way down the stairs.

"See you," says Bru.

"Why does Skooshie think you need your eyes checked?" Kit asks, as soon as we're in the lift.

"It was just a joke."

"They think you didn't see something properly. Was it Lemur?"

That's annoying too, how good Kit is at working stuff out.

"Yeah, OK," I admit. "I thought I saw him coming down the hill this morning. But then he didn't show up at the house."

"And he said it wasn't him?"

"Well, he just kept going on about how that wasn't the plan, we were supposed to meet at the den, blah, blah, blah, like I was a total numpty. But if it was a trick, why didn't he say so? The others laughed at me but they'd have thought Lemur managing to make me wait and wait was funnier. The problem is he's so good at telling stories, so convincing. We've stopped even wondering what's true and what's made up. I mean, look how scared Skooshie was at his ghost story."

"You weren't scared?"

"It was spooky – but in a good way. I wasn't scared, not like I thought it was real."

"The funny thing is," says Kit, "I saw him too."

"This morning? Really?"

"When you rushed out, I went to the window to see why. I saw him just coming into our flats. I don't think he'd seen you – he wasn't hurrying or anything... I did tell you he was weird!"

That night when we're in bed, I tell Kit everything that happened (she murmurs appreciation at the King Kong detail and sympathises about me not having the sword idea earlier).

"So either he sneaked back down—"

"Not in the lift – it was still there."

"...using the stairs. Or he went into Mr Murphy's house."

"I don't think so. Though Mr Murphy did want to see him."

"What?"

"Yeah, one night we were playing Kick the Can and Mr Murphy came out and said, 'Tell your pal to come and see me.'"

"He was really angry with Lemur that time at the lift, wasn't he?"

"Yeah. I wondered if he wanted to apologise? I told Lemur, but he just acted all, 'Yeah, right. Some chance I'm going to do that.' I never thought he'd go."

"But if Mr Murphy just wanted to apologise, wouldn't

Lemur have told you?" asks Kit. "What's going on there, then?"

I'm drifting off when Kit's voice comes out of the dark again. "Hey, Midge. What if the lift door had opened and you'd leapt out and it was Mr Murphy, not Lemur?"

I'm sinking so fast into sleep I nearly don't get the picture. Then the giggles hit both of us right at the same time.

A warning voice comes from the hall. "You two, settle down!"

I have to bury my face in the pillow to try and muffle the noise. Kit has a corner of sheet stuffed in her mouth. She pulls it out and sits up, suddenly sober. "Old folk don't have heart attacks if that happens, do they?"

"Not the ones from the Glasgow Corporation Factory," I say. "They're really tough. *They're made in Scotland. From girders.*"

And that sets her off again.

18

I've just put the last bit of toast in my mouth when Kit bellows from the living room, *"MIDGE!* THEY'RE GOING TO PLAY IT *NEXT* – C'MON!"

I scramble into place. She's pushed the coffee table out of the way to give us space to dance. She's turned up the radio really loud. Mum's sitting on the settee, ready to watch the performance. She's brave.

"Me first, then you," says Kit, getting into position. "Then both of us together. Right?"

"Right."

It starts. We shimmy from side to side during the intro and verse, hitting the disco beat. The chorus comes quick. We're off.

"**Shake, shake, shake...**" Kit throws her hips madly from side to side.

Then me, "**Shake, shake, shake...**" grooving with even more energy (and style).

"**Shake your booty – Shake your booty.**" Deeper swaying motions for this bit. Kit and I sing along, bumping hips together. The trumpets come in, underlining each command and giving our dance moves the kind of fanfare they deserve. And straight into the chorus again, "*Aw, shake, shake, shake...*"

The verses are really short. Here comes the chorus again – you've got to be ready to shake! We use the long *Aw* at the start to get into position, bum tilted to the left. This is my kind of dancing.

Aw, shake, shake, shake...
Shake, shake, shake...
Shake your booty,
Shake your booty!

To make the performance even more memorable, we spin round, reverse shimmy up to the settee and shake our booties in Mum's face. She shrieks with laughter, hitting out at our bums. "You cheeky monkeys!"

"*Aw, don't fight the feeling!*" Kit sings, and we both pull Mum into the dance arena. She's already laughing so much she can hardly stand, let alone dance. But we sing, "*Shake! ... Shake!*" really loudly at her and she has to join in.

"You're not a bad dancer, Mum," I say admiringly when the DJ fades the music so that he can entertain everybody with his chat again.

"Thank you," she says, dropping onto the settee.

"For an old person," I say with a grin.

"Oh, and there goes August's pocket money. What a shame!"

"Could we buy the record, Mum, so we can listen to it when we want? They don't play it often enough on the radio."

"Have you got any money to buy it?"

"No."

"Well, we'll see. It's not that long till Christmas, I suppose."

"*Christmas?*"

"We'll see. Right – are we ready to go?

It's surprising I'm in such a good mood when you think about it. We're having a Family Day Out. That's how my mum announced it yesterday, *three* capital letters. This was her way of telling us that all argument against it would be useless. Does she not realise? Does she not know how unfair she's being? I was halfway into a big moan about having other much more important things to do when I was stopped in my tracks by the realisation that I didn't have a story ready if she asked what. I could hardly tell her this was our day for Cathkin – so I shut up quick. (She thought it was the warning glint in her eyes that stopped me.) So here I am, about to waste an entire day with my family and we've had to postpone Cathkin YET AGAIN.

When I told them, Lemur gave me a look like I really had my priorities all wrong. Hector took out his chewed pencil and, with a weary sigh, edited The List. Skooshie punched me on the arm in what I think was sympathy (it hurt). Bru just said it would be even better when we did eventually get there. "'When?'" I heard Lemur mutter. "I think you mean 'if'." I don't much care what Lemur thinks – I'm still annoyed with him for lying. But I do feel bad for the rest of them. Really bad.

I'm trying not to think about what I'm missing. (Will they be hanging out in the den? Will they go to the park, to check out the dead soldiers in the boating pond? *Will they go to Cathkin without me?* The thought's unbearable, so I push it out of my head.)

We don't *ever* go out as a family, not unless we have to or we're on holiday – and that's different because then there aren't other things you could be doing. We're not going on holiday this year. No one's saying why but I think it might be something to do with the Grammar and the cost of the uniform and all the books I need. Kit must have been warned when I wasn't around because she hasn't complained about it, not even once. Anyway, I reckon that's why Mum's decided we're going out today. Kit's quite excited. I'm resigned. My dad's just looking bemused.

"So where are we going?" I ask. We're in the car and my dad's just turned left at the bottom of the hill.

"Kelvingrove Art Gallery," says Kit. How come she knows and I don't?

"Is that the place with the stuffed animals?" I say. Maybe this won't be as bad as I thought.

I really like the art gallery. It's got loads of interesting stuff in it, not just boring paintings. And the building is brilliant. The first great thing is that it is back to front. (Hector told me.) The builders did it the wrong way round, so the big grand entrance is at the back, looking at the park instead of at the main road. Or maybe it was the architect who got his drawing wrong. I'm not a hundred percent sure who was to blame, but whatever happened, the architect was so gutted that he jumped off one of the towers and killed himself. Total over-reaction, if you ask me. I mean, unless you know somebody like Hector, who would even notice it's the wrong way round?

The other great thing about the building is that inside it's one huge big high hall, open right up to the roof – the kind of place that *wants* you to shout your head off, so that you can hear your voice bounce off the walls and the ceiling. I wouldn't mind being locked in a museum overnight – me, Bru, Skooshie, Hector – I might even invite Lemur. There'd be the whole who-can-shout-loudest challenge. I'd also want to climb up the giant stuffed animals, especially a really tall one, like the giraffe. And sleeping in the same room as an Egyptian mummy has always been an ambition of mine.

Kit wanders by as I'm looking up at the ceiling and trying to judge just how loud I could sound. She prods me in the back and scoots off, with a muffled giggle. So that's her game! Secret chases round the museum – the double challenge of catching her and not being caught messing about? She's on!

It lasts until I trip over the edge of a display and nearly decapitate a stuffed penguin. Kit pretends she's got nothing to do with me, giving a loud tut of disapproval and disappearing. I think I've managed to escape a row by exiting sharpish and finding a great big fish in a display case to stare at, as though I'm totally fascinated. It turns out to be a pike and it is pretty interesting. It's not even a whole fish – just the head, which somehow works even better. The skin's dried out to give the pike's face the look of an alien. The lower jaw juts out and up over the upper jaw and you can see a range of sharp, spiky, vicious teeth. The upper jaw sort of snarls at you. And the eye is pure dead evil-looking. It's brilliant!

Dad turns up and bends down to peer at the pike too.

"They reckon the whole pike might have weighed about as much as Kit. That would make a lot of fish suppers," he says.

I laugh and turn to go.

"Jamie," says my dad, without even looking round.

"Yes, Dad?"

"Mind the penguins."

"Sorry, Dad."

I decide to go up to the first floor. It's full of paintings, so I'm not too optimistic about the fun value. (Is *anybody* that interested in pictures showing bowls of fruit?) I find my mum peering at a picture of Jesus being crucified – he's all lit up in a dark sky, his head bowed. She's silent for once, probably wondering what to make of it.

I look as well. I like it. I like it because he looks like a superhero, biding his time – like at any minute, his head's going to jerk up and he'll fix you with death-ray eyes... I don't share this thought with her though. I have a feeling she wouldn't appreciate it. Instead I say, "Very nice," then slope off to join my dad and Kit.

They're looking at a painting of Mary, Queen of Scots' execution. Not of her actually getting executed (disappointingly), but a few minutes before the chop.

Time's frozen – everything is just about to happen.

"D'you know, Dad, it took two goes with the axe to cut off her head?"

"Really? The story I've heard is that after she was dead the people saw her dress move. It turned out she had her wee pet dog hidden underneath it."

"Aw," says Kit. "So that she didn't go to the execution all on her own?"

"Yeah."

"What would've happened if she'd won the Battle of Langside, Dad?"

"Well, she stays Queen of Scotland. She brings up her son, James. Let's say she lives for a long time, to the same age as Elizabeth. Well, that would mean she's still alive when Elizabeth dies."

"So Mary becomes Queen of England too?"

"Yeah. What happens then? Does she move to London like her son James did when he became King of England? Or does she rule from Scotland?"

"She stays here," I say firmly. "She stays here and the whole country supports her."

"Then the whole history of Scotland is changed," says my dad. "We'd be the ones in charge."

"Could that have happened, d'you think, Dad?"

"I quite like it as an idea..."

I'm wandering on – there's only so much time you can spend looking at a painting. I'm not really paying that much attention. My eye skims over the pictures, snagging on details here and there – a bloke in a beard who reminds me of Billy Connolly, some horses whose legs look too skinny to keep them upright, some fruit, some more fruit and even more fruit... And then something really catches my attention. It's a word, not a picture. And the word is *Lorredan*!

It's on a painting – it's the title: *Mount Lorredan House, Glasgow, c. 1820.* The picture shows a big house and the grounds around it – it's exactly as Lemur described it. I don't mean more or less like he described it – I mean *exactly*. It looks so familiar to me from his story that I go up close and scrutinise the whole painting, wondering if I'll see Christy and Robert. I don't – but I do find something that sends a shiver down my spine. I recognise The Tree. You can just see the tree house, its wooden boards visible behind the leaves. And what's that, almost camouflaged against the browns and greens?

It's a rope, hanging down from a branch. Right there. And as I look, it seems like it's still swaying...

19

I'm playing tennis on my own. The advantage of this is that you get to hit a lot. I'm doing backhand after backhand, to perfect it. It's early and there's nobody else out. Hector's off somewhere with his parents today and Skooshie's visiting his gran. I've got into a really good rhythm: strings, wall, ground; strings, wall ground. Pling, dunk, dunk. Pling, dunk, dunk. I'll give it ten minutes longer, then go and get Bru.

Just as I'm hitting my 29th backhand in a row, he appears from the flats, in the company of his mum and the Toaty Terrors. The Toaty Terrors are busy pretending to be bees. At least I think that's why they're buzzing.

"Hey," Bru says, without his usual enthusiasm. "I've got to go shopping. School uniform. Sorry."

"Aw, well. I'll see you later." I kick a small stone towards him. "Here."

I watch them go down the hill to the bus stop, Bru kicking the stone, alternately using his left foot, then his right. He pauses to give me a wave at the corner, then goes back to kicking. I return to my backhand practice.

"Hey." I know it's Lemur but I'm still half-annoyed with him – half-annoyed but also half-desperate to talk about the picture. Well, half-desperate and half-reluctant to give him the satisfaction of knowing I'm half-desperate. (Wait a minute, those fractions aren't right – you can't have your feelings in three halves. You know what I mean – it's not worth working it out more accurately. But if it was, it would probably involve fifths. Say, $2/5$ annoyed, $2/5$ desperate and $1/5$ reluctant to indulge him? Yeah.)

So I keep playing like I haven't heard him. He sits on the steps and watches. I go in to really smack a forehand, but mistime it and the ball shoots off the frame at a wild angle. Lemur leaps in the air and catches it one-handed. It's so cool that a good $1/5$ of my annoyance converts itself into admiration.

He can tell. He grins and throws the ball back to me.

"Hey," I say.

I sit down beside him and put my racquet on the ground.

"We missed you yesterday," he says. "How was your Family Day Out?"

"Surprisingly interesting. I saw the house in your story."

"What?"

"Mount Lorredan House."

"You can't have. It's gone."

"I know that! I saw it in a painting at the museum. That's where we went."

"Oh. What did it look like?"

"Exactly like you described it. I thought you must've seen the picture and used it to make up your story."

He grins. "Sometimes you make stuff up and sometimes you don't."

"You're good at making stuff up," I say.

"Thanks."

"It's not a compliment. In fact, another word for 'making stuff up' is 'lying'. You're good at lying."

"I never lie."

"You did about being in my flats the other day."

"No, I didn't. Did I say I hadn't been there? No. I just didn't say that I *had* been there."

"So you admit you were!"

"Sorry. I didn't want the others to know."

"Why not? What were you doing?"

"I went to see that Murphy bloke."

"You told me you weren't going to go."

Lemur pauses, like he's not sure whether to go on. Then the words come out in a rush. "I know – and that's what I believed when I said it. Then I thought about what you would do in the same situation. You're not a coward – you would have gone."

"You were scared about going to see him?" This is amazing. Lemur is frightened of nothing.

"A bit. I didn't know what to expect."

"He was kind of... angry the other day. You could have told us. We'd've gone with you."

"I thought I had to do it on my own."

"So you went. What happened?"

"He said he'd wanted to talk to me ever since that day at the lift. He had a friend, a long, long time ago, when he was young. With fair hair, blue eyes—"

"Yeah, it did look like he thought you were somebody

he knew. Why was he so angry at his pal? What was it he said? 'Give it back!' What was all that about?"

Lemur shrugs. "I didn't ask him. It must have been important at the time."

"It's a long time to bear a grudge. What else did he say?"

"Well, then he started talking about all the stuff he used to do when he was young, how he was a big Third Lanark fan. He told me the names of the players – he knew them all, the positions they played."

"That must've been interesting," I say. "To hear about it from somebody who was actually there."

"And then... And then... he *started to cry.*"

"What? Actually cry?"

Lemur nods.

"What did you do?"

Lemur bites his lip. For once he looks unsure of himself. "I ran away," he confesses. "I had no idea what to do, so I just left him. Sitting there, crying... You wouldn't have done that, Midge."

Wouldn't I? I don't know. Grown-ups crying – it feels all wrong. It's a bit scary. I quite like Lemur thinking I'm better than him though.

"Well, it was a shame he was upset," I say, "but maybe you did him some good going to visit him."

"I don't think so."

"Old people like thinking about the past. Though I think they should keep their crying for when they're on their own. What could you have done to help him?"

"Nothing," Lemur admits. "I was planning to come

and get you after I saw him, honest, but I felt too bad. I just wanted to get away."

He looks at me. I think he wants sympathy.

"You great big girl's blouse," I say.

That makes him laugh. Luckily. "Den?" he says.

"Den," I agree.

The den's more or less dried out since the unexpected deluge during the storm last week. And did I mention that it's been improved? Bru arrived one day with both arms around the base of a large lamp. The lampshade totally obscured his face – it's a wonder he managed to cross Prospecthill Road without being run over.

"My next-door neighbour put it out," he said. "It's OK," he adds, misinterpreting our silence. "She said I could take it."

But we weren't quiet because we were sitting there suspecting Bru had nicked it. And it wasn't because we were wondering how to point out, without hurting Bru's feelings, the obvious drawback that we have no electricity. The reason was we were speechless with amazement. How could anybody throw out something so fantastic?

Because this is no ordinary lamp. It's the base that's the exciting part. It's a pale green bottle on its side. And inside the bottle... is a ship! An actual ship, carved out of wood, with three big masts. The sails are unfurled – all huge and white and billowy, like it's just waiting to catch a breeze and go.

"Wow!" said Lemur.

"Is it a galleon?" I asked.

"Yeah..." said Hector vaguely.

"So how do they do that then, get it in through the tiny opening in the bottle?" asked Skooshie. He was right to ask. What we were looking at there was a total impossibility.

"They don't have to," said Lemur. "They make the ship first, then they make the bottle round it."

"No, they don't," said Bru. "It's actually a trick. The ship is small enough to go through the bottle opening, but the glass is special magnifying glass, so when the ship gets in, it looks much bigger."

"Really? Wouldn't it have to be a pure midget ship and incredibly powerful glass?"

Then I said, "They're both wrong, Skooshie. The ship's built *inside* the bottle."

"Inside? But you couldn't get your fingers through the opening."

"You don't need to. It's built by toaty wee boat-building pixies..." I only escape a smack for this because Bru has warned us how fragile the bottle is and Skooshie is wary of violent gestures in its vicinity.

"Hector," pleaded Skooshie, despairing of ever knowing the truth.

Hector was only waiting to be asked: "They build the ship so that the wooden bit fits through the bottle opening. And they design the masts so that they can fold down. They attach string to the masts. They pop the ship into the bottle, then use the string to pull up the masts once it's in there."

"Aw. Clever..."

So here we are, Lemur and I, sprawling on the settee cushions and admiring our impossible ship-in-a-bottle lamp. Lemur's produced a packet of sweets from his pocket – those brilliant new ones, Trebor Double Agents. He's got the strawberry and cream flavour, Spy number 004 (good choice). With just two of us, the packet lasts a surprisingly long time.

"That lamp's just brilliant," I say.

"It is," Lemur agrees wholeheartedly. "It's possibly the most impressive thing I've ever seen."

"Know what you mean," I say. "Good old Bru."

"What a find."

"Yeah, it's the finishing touch."

"Exactly," says Lemur. "This is officially the best den ever."

"Definitely. And haunted. Not everybody can say that about their den."

He catches the sarcasm in my tone and grins.

"You don't believe in ghosts?"

Do I or don't I? It's something we've not had a serious discussion about. I think I want to. But I'm not totally convinced I actually do.

"Not really," I admit. "Which is a pity – unless you're Skoosh, of course."

"Is it? Ghosts aren't that interesting – all see-through and whiney and never able to join in. Always watching from the sidelines. Never getting picked. I couldn't be doing with that."

"Even Christy? I thought he sounded like a lot of fun."

"Yeah. Hard for a ghost to be a member of the gang though."

"But I did like your story, honest. It was brilliant! And I wish we did have a den ghost, one just like Christy."

"But I wasn't lying, Midge. Christy really did live here, you know."

"So you say..."

"I can prove it. C'mon." He stands up and starts hauling the settee cushions away from the base of the tree. I jump up before I'm tipped off. "The story says Christy carved something on the tree."

"Yeah, I remember."

"Let's see then," he says. "If I pull it back, can you get in to take a look?"

"Yeah."

Lemur uses his foot to push back the green stuff around the foot of the tree.

"Anything?" he says.

"There's a hollow. It's a bit dark... Ooof! This is when my torch would be useful. If Kit hadn't used up the batteries."

I'm crouching down, squinting into the darkness.

"No. Nothing here," I say.

"Look harder."

I reach in. My fingers feel something rough against the smoothness of the tree.

"Push it back a bit further," I say.

Then I can just make it out. Writing.

ROBERT
MISSED BY CHRISTY

"Believe me now?" says Lemur.

"Wow," I say.

We stay in the den for a while. It's quiet without the others. Our conversation is missing that competitive feel, when everybody is trying to out-funny each other. There's a bit of a breeze and the leaves of the tree are rustling above our heads. I'm on the alert for evidence of Christy-as-ghost, but it just sounds like leaves rustling, to be honest.

"If Christy is here," I say, "what's keeping him here? Kit asked me."

"You told her?" says Lemur.

"Yeah – we'd already told my dad, so I thought it was OK."

"What did she think?"

"She loved hearing the story. She couldn't wait to find out how it ended. And now she's desperate to get into the den, to see for herself – I made it perfectly clear that's never going to happen."

"What did you say, about Christy?"

"I said I wasn't sure."

"Do you think it has something to do with feeling guilty about his brother?" Lemur asks.

"No, I don't. It wasn't Christy's fault that Robert fell. When you do something like that, you've decided to do it – you can't blame anybody else if it goes wrong."

"I agree. So what do you think the reason is?"

"Maybe it's not that Christy's forced to be here. Maybe he chooses to be. Maybe he just doesn't want to go. There's too much going on for him to leave."

Lemur grins. "I like that idea," he says. "Maybe he's having too much fun. Perhaps your dad's right – perhaps Christy's our kind of ghost!"

We have a really good time, talking about Christy and imagining what he's like. Then I have to head home for lunch. We're just leaving the den when Lemur says, "Midge, can we keep it a secret?"

"What? The carving? Aw, no, Lemur – they're going to love seeing it! Though it might tip Skooshie over the edge."

"No – the whole Murphy thing."

"I'm not lying to them!"

"I'm not saying lie – if they ask you, then tell them. But if they don't, just let it go. Please."

It doesn't feel right. I don't normally keep stuff from the others. But it looks like this is important to Lemur. And when you think about it, it's not really my story to tell.

"OK," I say, a bit reluctantly.

"I can always rely on you, Midge," he says.

I have to push him into a bush, just to relieve the tension.

"Yeah – always," I say, and I'm off, sprinting down May Terrace before he can get out of the bush.

20

Finally. *You* know what I mean. It's Friday. *Friday.*

I'm looking for a grey t-shirt that I never wear. This turns out to be a mistake, as it attracts unwanted attention.

"I've never known you be so particular about what you're wearing. Is there a girl involved?" asks my mum.

"Mum!" I'm disgusted that she could even think it.

"If there is, I think this red one would be better."

"I want the grey one." I can't, of course, explain to her that I'm looking for something that will not stand out against the green of the pitch or the muddy brown of the rain-and-rust-marked concrete of the stand. If I blend in, I will be harder to spot from a distance. If I wear red, I'll stand out like a traffic light.

"Stop pulling everything out the drawer. Here – I'll get it."

She looks doubtful when I appear in the kitchen wearing the grey t-shirt.

"Is it not a bit small?"

"No – it's good." I stretch it down as I reach up for a bowl in the cupboard, to avoid an exposure of belly.

As we have breakfast, I concentrate on flexing my arm muscles silently in an attempt to loosen the tight grip of the sleeves round them. I don't want to keel over if they cut off the supply of blood to my brain.

"Are you constipated?" asks Kit, staring at me in surprise.

"Shut – up!" I growl at her.

We spend the day playing tennis. We don't put a lot of energy into it – we need to save that. For once nobody cares who wins. When we're done with that, we lie in the grass reviewing the plan. We speak in voices so low that there's no chance of passing on any actual information to each other. So it's a good job we've had the plan in place for a long time.

Only dinner to get through now.

Thursday is crispy pancake day, all year round. My mum tries to introduce different food in the summer, salads and stuff like that, and she's welcome to, just not on Thursdays. Kit and I won't have it. Chicken and mushroom is our favourite. I like Bru's idea of moving time about, but if I was offered a superpower I think I'd go for the ability to make stuff bigger. Like insects (think of the fun you could have in class with that one!). Like my boat on the boating pond at the park (just mine – I'd leave the others the right size). Like wee dogs that are being barked at by big dogs. Like me. But I'd start with crispy pancakes, because they are ridiculously small, even for Kit. They disappear in a flash. I'd do her a crispy pancake the size of her whole plate. Mine would be the size of the table. It's a happy thought.

But today I'm so excited and nervous, not even a crispy pancake can make me feel hungry. I play with mine in a distracted way, using my knife to squish out the filling.

"You not hungry?" my mum says suspiciously. In a minute she'll be feeling my forehead and dosing me with some of that disgusting pink medicine that will make me sleepy.

"Just wondering how they make these," I say, trying to sound like a boy who is a walking miracle of health. I bounce my knife off the pancake surface. "Clever, aren't they? How they keep all that sauce inside?" Then I eat the whole thing in two enormous mouthfuls, making "Yum!" noises to show how much I'm enjoying it. Trying to do both things at once causes me to choke. My mum just shakes her head, but it looks like I've managed to escape the horrible medicine.

We meet up inside the back entrance to my flats, which is tucked in too far to be visible from our window.

"Now for the tricky part," I say. "Somebody needs to retrieve the jemmy and prise the iron sheet away."

"Already done," says Hector.

"How?"

"I did it last night, when it was dark," says Lemur.

"We didn't want to attract attention by doing it now," says Hector.

"Are you sure? It doesn't look like it'll open."

"That was the idea – we didn't want it to look

tampered with. Watch. Agent 1!" hisses Hector. (It was his idea to give us all code names.)

Lemur darts across the road and up the grass. The iron sheet pulls away easily and within seconds he's out of sight.

"Agent 2!" That's me. The corrugated iron is a deep-rust red. I have time to study it while I'm waiting for the others – Skooshie, then Bru, with Hector bringing up the rear. In less time than we could have imagined, we're all inside, ready for Phase Two.

We creep through the overgrown grass and weeds on the outside of the embankment. Skooshie has volunteered to take the lead – he's going at the vegetation with his arms like an explorer hacking his way through the African jungle. We pause in a particularly dark patch where there are trees to give us cover. It's just the other side of the fence from the place where we made the Cathkin Berry Wine. It's a whole new world. Before we can stop him, Lemur has scrambled up the embankment.

He turns and gestures. "Come and look!"

We risk it. We clamber up the steep slope and peer over the top. In front of us the terracing falls in regular steps, down to a very short, white wall. Beyond the wall, the green of the pitch extends forever.

"Wow!"

We slide back down the slope and keep going. The undergrowth is denser now. We have to come part way up the embankment sometimes just to find a path through. We keep crouched down, trying to blend in. I was dead right about the grey t-shirt.

Finally we're out of the undergrowth and looking across at the stand a short way off – just a piece of open grass between us and it.

"Ready?" says Hector. We sprint in turns, the same order as before. When I collapse beside Lemur, he's lying back looking up into the rusting roof above us.

"At last," he murmurs.

We sit, surveying the park and feeling triumphant at our achievement. And then it's time to explore.

"Look – you can see where the turnstiles were!"

"Can you imagine the crowds of people queuing to get in?"

"Look! Look at me! I'm running onto the pitch *right where the players came on!*"

"Can't you hear them shouting to their team mates? 'HERE – HERE – PASS!'"

Up close, I can sort of see why my mum went on about it being pretty dangerous. It's been so neglected over the years that it's falling apart. We need to jump over the holes, leap to safe ground as surfaces crumble away beneath our feet. We climb up exposed girders, competing to see who can get the highest (Lemur and Skooshie, who both continue to claim victory, even after Hector officially declares it's a draw). The creak of the roof is not exactly reassuring.

It's absolutely magic.

I stop hiding, stop worrying that we'll be spotted. I mean, I haven't forgotten I'll be in big trouble if I am. But I'm realising that whatever happens, it will be worth it.

"Wouldn't this be a great place to have a sword fight?" says Bru, as we run up and down the terracing on the far side. "Think of François, up against six Spaniards, leaping about, bamboozling them all, cutting off the edges of their ridiculous moustaches with a quick flash of his blade."

"I've always wondered why it's not pronounced 'swurd', like 'word'," says Hector. "Swurd fighting. I am François," he adds in a ridiculous French accent, "the best swurd fighter in all of France!"

"Because that would be abswurd," says Lemur with a grin. We groan.

"It's because swurd fighting is something totally different," I say. "It's when you're so amazingly brilliant, you don't need weapons. When you just hurl cleverly worded insults at your enemy and *crush* him with those."

"On guard," says Hector.

We take up a fight stance.

"MONSIEUR, YOU ARE A **FOOL**!" I thrust forward with an imaginary sword as I shout it.

"AND YOU, MONSIEUR, ARE A **BRAGGART**!"

Murmurs of appreciation from the others as Hector flings this at me. I laugh it off, François-style: "**HA, HA, HA, HA!**"

"Your farts, monsieur, smell of flowers."

Hector staggers back, as though hit hard. He tries to rally.

"Your face, monsieur, looks like a Wagon Wheel... That somebody has chewed."

I flinch and clutch my shoulder. A hit, but not a fatal one.

I step in for the kill. Time for something special.

"Do me the honour, monsieur, of admitting that you play football like a girl!"

"I'm a goner..." croaks Hector. He staggers about for a bit, then slumps over the white wall that runs around the pitch.

He waits for the whoops of appreciation to die down, then rights himself and says, "Actually I don't – and you know it. And if we had a ball, I'd prove it."

We don't hear what Lemur says, as he runs off in the direction of the stand. He reappears in a minute, clutching a football.

"Where did you get that?"

He grins. "I threw it over the fence yesterday morning."

"Aw, cool move, Lemur!"

We take turns defending, attacking and in goal. And I am proud to tell you that we play the football of our lives. I don't know if it's because of the pitch. On the grass you bounce – it's like running with springs on your feet after the skitey orange grit of the recs. Or maybe it's because we're inspired, playing in the very place where all those Third Lanark players sprinted and passed and shot, where they won their matches – and lost some – years and years ago.

I'm running faster than I've ever run before, the ball at my feet. I boot it up the field to Skooshie – a long, perfect punt. I watch him racing into the sun, Lemur and Bru trying to fend him off, Hector hopping about on the goal line. And maybe I'm imagining it, but in the sunlight, in the blur of movement, it looks like they're all wearing red.

With each goal, we turn, arms spread wide, to accept the applause in the stand – *HIGH, HIGH, HIGH!*

It's good that Cathkin sees us at our best. It's right. We

don't know it, but this turns out to be the last game of football we ever play together.

I can't help glancing occasionally at our living-room window, just once or twice. There's no one there. As I'd hoped, the blinds are pulled down against the evening sun.

But somebody is watching. One floor above, Mr Murphy is standing at his window. I don't want to make Lemur feel bad by reminding him of the other day, so I don't say anything. I just hope seeing us brings back some nice memories for the old bloke.

Hector, Skooshie and Bru are all still totally absorbed in the game. Lemur's having a rest on the grass at the side of the pitch. He's staring at the stand like he can't believe we're actually here. He grins at me when I throw myself down beside him.

"As good as you thought, Lemur?"

"Better!"

The others get tired eventually and come to join us. The sun's dropping in the sky and we'll have to go soon. We're making the most of our last few minutes.

Hector reaches forward and captures a spider that's on his sandshoe.

"That one's been there since we were in the stand," he says, impressed. "Showing the amazing power of the spider to cling on, whatever happens... How many spiders d'you reckon there are in this whole park?"

We consider.

"Loads," says Bru. This sounds likely and we all nod in agreement.

"I ate a spider once," says Skooshie, randomly.

Hector, Bru and I snort with laughter. The

announcement is news to Lemur. You forget sometimes that he hasn't always been around.

"Ate a spider? When?"

"Primary 2, I think. I was tricked."

"You weren't tricked into eating the spider, Skoosh," says Hector. "You were the one who suggested the spider-eating, if I remember correctly. You were tricked into eating it *alone*."

"Yeah," Skooshie admits. "We agreed we'd do it on three – one, two, three, spider down the hatch – we had a spider each, we weren't sharing. So one, two, three – I'm crunching, I'm swallowing—"

"And we're just looking at him, totally amazed he could have believed we'd ever do it!" says Bru, laughing.

"All for one and one for all, and all that," Skooshie protests.

"Yeah, but that doesn't mean you do just anything. Did you really think it was a good plan, spiders for lunch?"

Skooshie gives a huge grin. "Not really. But I had an idea it would make me a legend!"

"And it did!" says Hector. "Everybody at school talked about you for weeks! We seriously considered changing your nickname to Spiderboy."

"Why didn't we?" asks Bru.

"He was too disappointed in the outcome," I say. "It didn't give you the superpowers you hoped for, did it, Skoosh?"

Skooshie shakes his head, slightly regretful. Then he perks up. "Spiderboy – done before though. The Mighty Skoosh – a one-off!"

"You're right there," I say.

We walk back across the pitch. Up and over the embankment, and out through the corrugated iron fencing.

Skooshie, Hector and Lemur head off up the hill. Slowly, because Skooshie's got the jemmy down his sock and up his t-shirt again. Bru and I walk towards the flats. We hear them talking as they go.

"I'd have eaten the spider with you, Skooshie," Lemur's saying.

"I know you would, Lemur," says Skooshie. He gives Lemur a friendly shove in appreciation and they disappear into the darkness.

21

And the next day ...

Well, it feels a bit flat.

And it doesn't happen gradually, not like a soft bike tyre that slowly lets you down. Oh no. When this happens, it's more like a balloon going

A big "What do we do now?" cloud blocks out the sun. No one has the answer, not even Hector.

The day starts off well enough.

We're sitting in the den and we are full of it. First of all, we seem to have got away with the whole thing. If my mum knew anything about our exploit – or even suspected anything, there are people living on the outskirts of Edinburgh who would've heard her shouting. But not a peep. We've actually managed to pull it off!

We re-live the whole Cathkin experience, loads of times, chipping in with all the details. We each do a Top

Three list of favourite moments. Playing on the pitch is picked by everybody.

"Yeah, nice one planking the ball, Lemur!"

"What about you, Bru? Top absolute favourite?"

"It was all brilliant," Bru sighs. "But maybe the best bit was lying back in the stand and hearing the Cathkin roar in my head, thousands and thousands of people cheering."

"Aw, fantastic..."

"You know that kind of noise that you can feel in your chest? It just seems to fill up your whole body?"

"Yeah."

"*SUPER-BRU!   SUPER-BRU!   SUPER-BRU!*" Skooshie improvises.

Bru gives him a grin and a thumbs-up of appreciation.

We spread our souvenirs out in the centre of the den. These are mainly fragments found in or chipped off the stand. Maybe they wouldn't look too impressive to an outsider – weird-shaped lumps of crumbling concrete, random chunks of wood, a bendy wedge of rusty corrugated iron – but if you know their story, you know their true value. All totally priceless, because we'd never give them up, not for anything.

So we're all talking at once, getting louder and more animated as we remember extra things. We're totally buzzing – agreeing and debating and laughing. Then suddenly we're like those toy bunnies in the adverts, the ones that play the drums. Not the one that keeps on going, forever and ever. We're the ones whose batteries have run out of juice and we've stopped with one arm in the air, lacking the oomph to even bring it down.

Lemur's actually quiet – that's how bad things are.

"It's just," says Skooshie, "that it was so *good*."

"Yeah. Nothing will ever be that good again. Ever. Will it?"

"No..."

"We can't do nothing."

"We need to do something."

"Yeah..."

"What about The List, Hector?"

Hector rummages in his pocket. He pulls out the scrap of paper and unscrunches it. It's become more grey than white in colour and it's been scribbled on so much I think only Hector can decipher it now.

We wait as his eyes flick down, his expression staying gloomy. Then he makes an exaggerated *pfff*! noise, like he's lost all hope.

"Nothing," he says.

"We need to do something," says Bru. "There's not that much of the holidays left—"

"BRU!" This is the worst thing anybody has said yet.

"I know, I know. But it's true. We've got to make the most of the time we've got left."

"Is there really nothing on The List at all, Hector?"

Hector looks again. He knows we're depending on him.

"Well," he says, "we could go to the park?"

"We could borrow somebody's dog and take it to the park for a walk," I suggest.

"No dogs," says Skooshie firmly.

"Aw, Skoosh..."

To be honest, I'd forgotten about Skooshie's dog

phobia. We used to take people's dogs for a walk quite a lot but then there was an incident when one of them bit Skooshie. Well, Shep didn't really *bite* him. We were rolling down the hill in the park and he just got a bit excited – Shep, not Skooshie – and thought part of the game was to grab hold of Skooshie's leg. It was more of a playful nip than a bite, though the way Skooshie tells the story, you can actually hear the *Jaws* theme tune in the background.

Which is why Skooshie's not so keen on dogs any more. Doesn't matter how toaty they are – in fact, he says the wee ones are worse because of the way they bounce about and get at your ankles. At least you can see the big ones coming. That's maybe why he likes playing at the flats so much. We're not allowed dogs here. Or cats. I think in fact there might be a ban on pets of any kind. Though the McIntyres in our flats used to have a secret tortoise. That seemed like a safe kind of choice: it doesn't create much mess or noise and it's an easy one to disguise, if Glasgow Corporation send round any kind of Pet Spy. But it turned out that tortoises are harder to manage than you'd think. You know the thawing out thing you have to do to them after hibernation? I didn't know about it either, but apparently it's kind of important and the McIntyres didn't do it right, so poor old Speedy Gonzales bought it. But it was a whole month before they worked out it was dead – they just thought it was dozing. So, all kinds of drawbacks to having a tortoise as a pet. A lot less chance of being bitten by it while you're rolling down a hill, though.

"Absolutely no dogs," says Skooshie, like he's been following the whole dog-tortoise-dog chain in my head.

"Fair enough," I say.

"We could go round the doors and ask people for ginger bottles," he counter-suggests.

"What would we do with the bottles?" says Lemur, puzzled.

"Aw, Lemur, you're not one of those people that don't take their ginger bottles back, are you?"

"What are you talking about?"

"So you are. Let me explain. For every bottle you take back to the shop, you get some money. Enough bottles, there's enough money to get sweets, or more ginger, whatever you fancy."

"You pay a deposit on the bottle."

"No – they *give you* money."

"I get that – I mean, you've paid a deposit when you buy the ginger."

"I don't think so," says Skooshie. "This is free money."

"So you go to someone's door and ask them for their bottles and they give them to you?"

"People do," says Skooshie.

"That *is* free money," says Lemur, impressed.

"Some people don't," Skooshie feels obliged to add. "Some laugh and shut the door. Some shout and shut the door. A few swear at you – not that many though. You'd be surprised how many can't be bothered to take them back. We're like a public service."

"Let's do that," says Lemur, getting up. "If we do it in the flats, we'll be able to get round lots of doors without walking very far."

"Eh, no," says Bru.

"Why not?"

"My mum says it's just glorified begging. It's a total no-no in my house."

"Mine as well," I add.

Skooshie snorts. "Begging! Do your mothers not know a good business opportunity when they see it? C'mon – let's go and do it in my road."

"You're on!"

It turns out to be quite a successful venture. An hour and a half later and we're clinking our way to the Mount Florida Café with two full plastic bags.

Which makes you think. When we grow up, maybe Skooshie's the one of us who's going to make a fortune.

Over the next few days, we get back to normal. Bru's right – we can't afford to waste any time pining for what's been and thinking we'll never do anything to beat it. Cathkin fades slowly and magically into legend. And although it might be true that we'll never do anything quite so pure dead brilliant again, we have it to hold onto – something that totally fantastic and out of this world. It's there – shining – in our memories for whenever we need it.

Well, I say things get back to normal. In fact, they take a turn for the weird. The totally weird.

22

We're sitting in the den passing round a bottle of American cream soda that is nearly done. Our talk today is serious.

"I've never known anybody that's died," says Bru.

"Yeah, you have," says Hector. "D'you not remember Skooshie's cousin's other gran?"

Skooshie pauses in draining the last dregs of ginger from the bottle to contribute, "Yeah – her," then up-ends the bottle into his mouth again.

"Well, we never met her," says Bru. "Skooshie'd never even met her. But we met Mr Murphy – remember that day when he grabbed Lemur and had a go at him? We actually knew him quite well."

"It is spooky," agreed Hector. "Where is Lemur anyway?"

We were never there before him. "Must be planning a big entrance," I say.

"Oh," says Skooshie. "Should I have left him some cream soda? Ah well, never mind." He puts the empty bottle down. "Talk of the devil, here he is."

"Where've you been?"

"Just out and about. Then I went to get you, Midge."

He glances at me. This is to make up for the other day, the Mr Murphy day. And I've just announced to everybody that he's only late to be the centre of attention, which makes me feel a bit pish as a pal.

"You weren't in – but your sister was. She's really annoying, isn't she? She bombarded me with questions."

"What about?"

"Ghosts, dens... and school uniforms?"

Hector snorts. "Girls. Totally off their heads."

There's no space for Lemur on the cushions. He gets down on the ground, lying flat out and closing his eyes.

"Been running?" asks Hector.

"No. Just tired. What's happening?"

"I've got news," I say.

"About that Mr Murphy," says Skooshie before I can get started. "Remember that man in Midge's flats that was shouting and accusing you?"

"Oh, him. What about him?"

"He's dead!" says Hector.

"When?"

"Last night," I say loudly. This is my news and I'm not having them hijack it.

"So?"

"Well, we were just saying we don't know that many people who have died. So it's news."

"How did he die?"

"Midge jumped out at him when the lift opened and gave him a heart attack."

"Shut up, Hector. My mum says he died because he was lonely."

"People don't die because they're lonely," says Skooshie. With five brothers and sisters, Skooshie does not believe that loneliness exists.

"That's probably true," I admit. "My dad says he was just old."

"So, he was an old man and he died." Lemur shrugs.

This was my news and we were enjoying it before Lemur blundered in. Even though he's lying down and not bouncing around like usual, somehow he still does actually manage to make himself the centre of attention. Plus I'm surprised at his reaction. I'd thought Lemur would care. It's like the conversation we had the other day about Mr Murphy never happened. Like Lemur never visited him, never saw Mr Murphy crying. I'm so annoyed I hunch over and poke the ground, like I've discovered something really interesting down there.

And so I miss the start of it. By the time I tune in again there's a heated debate in full flow.

"Every four years," Bru's saying. "Every year is 365 and a quarter days long. The extra quarters add up to a day every four years. So there's a leap year every four years. Like this year."

"No, you're wrong there," says Hector. "Because a year is a bit *less* that 365 and a quarter days – just a toaty bit less. But over time that adds up. So some years when you're expecting a leap year, it doesn't happen."

"Like when?" Skooshie's very doubtful. "I've been watching out for leap years ever since I was born and they've never missed one yet. Every four years, regular as clockwork, like Bru says."

"So how many have you lived through?" says Hector,

less than impressed by the vastness of Skooshie's experience.

Skooshie does a bit of discreet counting on his fingers. "This will be my fourth. Wait a minute... I was born in 1964 but *after* the 29th of February – does that one still count?"

There's a general feeling that it does, that if there had been no leap day in the year of Skooshie's birth, somebody in his family would have mentioned it to him.

"OK – four, and they haven't missed one."

"They don't skip them that often," Hector explains. "Just three times every four hundred years."

"So how do you know when they're going to skip one?" asks Bru.

"It's the years ending in zero zero, when the century changes. You don't count three of them. So 1700, no leap year. 1800, no leap year. 1900, no leap year. 2000 leap year."

"So the 29th of February, 1900 didn't exist?" I say, because I've forgotten to still be annoyed. "Weird."

"No one was expecting it to," says Lemur, who's now propped up on one elbow and looking a bit livelier. "But there was a time when some days people were waiting for were actually lost."

"Lost?"

"Where?"

"How?"

"Well, a long time ago, they used to think like Bru – that you needed a leap year every four years. The extra days started adding up and making a difference. They realised that meant the link between the year and the seasons was getting broken. The date was slipping behind the season. By the eighteenth century, when the calendar said the 25th of March, the weather said the 6th of April."

"So if they'd kept going like that, we'd have ended up with Christmas in the summer?"

"Eventually," says Lemur.

"Like in Australia," says Hector, knowingly. His cousins live in Australia so he's something of an authority on the place.

"Would we have got kangaroos as well?"

Hector opens his mouth to respond to Skooshie's question but Lemur's not for any more interruptions. "So they decided," he continues loudly, "to change the calendar and miss out some days so the dates and the seasons matched again."

"How did that work?"

"In 1752 on the 2nd of September everyone went to sleep. And when they woke up, it was the 14th of September."

"So those days – the 3rd to the 13th – they just didn't exist?"

"No – they were lost."

"That's so weird... Can you imagine what that would feel like?"

"Some people thought the days had been stolen from them," says Lemur. "There were riots in the street!"

"People protesting that they wanted their eleven days back?"

"Yes – weren't they stupid?"

"Were they school days?" asks Bru. "*I* wouldn't be asking for those back!"

"They were just days," says Lemur. "What use were they? The people went to sleep, they woke up and it was later than they thought it would be. So what?"

"Well, what if something important fell on those days? My birthday's on the 10th of September – I'd've missed it."

"Yeah, it's not just the days that were lost. It's everything that might have happened on them."

"The same things just happened a few days later," says Lemur.

"Not in the same way. Take Hector's birthday. It just wouldn't feel the same celebrating it on the 14th."

"It *is* like having time nicked from you."

"Time's just time," says Lemur. "It didn't belong to them. How could it be stolen?"

He's getting red in the face. I can sense that no one's going to back down on this one. It could go on forever.

Then Bru comes to the rescue. "They were time thieves, you know," he says, his voice mysterious. "They didn't nick the days to fix the calendar. They nicked them to cover up what really happened then – things so strange that they couldn't allow anybody to remember them. It's been a secret for all this time. We're the only ones to have worked it out. And we owe it to the world to remember the things that actually happened, the things they tried to hide. You first, Midge."

I could see where he was going with this and I'm ready.

"You might have asked yourself whether the Loch Ness Monster is actually real..."

"TOO RIGHT SHE'S REAL!" hoots Skooshie, and he's backed up by a general hullaballoo of agreement.

"Well, you might have asked yourself what Nessie looks like..."

"Like this!" Skooshie, Bru and Hector do a three-man impersonation (or should that be im-monster-ation?) of Nessie, arching up out of the water. The sound effects are impressive: a cross between a tyrannosaurus rex in a bad mood and a zombie pig.

"Cool... Well, have you ever wondered how she got into Loch Ness?"

"That I have asked myself," Skooshie admits.

"Then let me tell you. It all happened on the 3rd of September, the first day to be nicked by the time thieves. At this time, Nessie lived in the River Clyde."

"The Clyde? Here in Glasgow? Isn't Loch Ness miles away?"

"Yeah, Midge, it definitely is."

"Maybe she got out and ran cross-country for part of it—"

"WILL YOU JUST SHUT UP AND LISTEN?"

"We're listening!" This in an aggrieved tone, like I'm being unreasonable.

"Her mother had been the very last of the dinosaurs – and before you ask, it was a type of dinosaur that hasn't been discovered yet. (Hey, Dinosaur Discoverer – that'd be such a cool job! I might put that on my list.) Anyway, she'd managed to hide an egg at the bottom of the Clyde. It stayed hidden for hundreds and thousands of years. Then one day there was a thaw after a freezing cold winter and the egg hatched...

"Nobody suspected the baby dinosaur was in the river. She ate fish and things like oranges that fell off the boats (she was especially keen on oranges), and she grew bigger and bigger. And at the same time the Clyde got busier and busier.

"So, there was Nessie, minding her business, just chasing a big juicy fish. In her excitement she bobbed up a bit too close to a boat. There was a shout – she'd been seen! They were after her! Some wanted to capture her, so they could sell her to a circus. Others wanted to kill her and make her into Nessie burgers."

"Aw, no!" says Skooshie, looking really anxious, even though he's got a fairly clear idea of how this one's going to end.

"She swam like she'd never swum before, desperate to escape. But in her panic she went inland instead of out to sea. The river got narrower and shallower, too shallow for Nessie – her front legs hit the riverbed. She couldn't swim any further! And she was too big and heavy to outrun them. But she didn't give up, not for a minute – because Scottish dinosaurs don't. There was one more thing she could try. Pushing up off her strong back legs, she reached for the sky. To the astonishment of everybody watching, the webbing on her front legs meant they worked as wings! There was nothing the chasers could do – just try and steady their boats against the blasts of wind from Nessie's flapping as she soared up into the sky and away."

"Yeah! Go, Nessie!"

"She flew until she found a nice big, deep loch to settle in. And that's where she's been since 1752. And sometimes she likes to play games by popping her head above the water and shouting, '*YOO HOO!*' to people with cameras on the banks."

"Good one, Midge..."

"My turn! On the 4th of September the people were awoken by a weird storm. The sky was raining Irn-Bru and throwing down hailstones made out of marshmallows..."

We talk on as the day disappears into the dark. There are so many fantastic impossible things to describe that really we could've easily filled a whole month of nicked days.

23

"Do you fancy," asks Lemur the next afternoon, "taking part in a ritual?" He's leaning back against the big tree in the den. He's the only one of us who looks like a normal human being at the moment. We've retired to the den because the heat outside is too much and the rest of us are red-faced and probably about to keel over with heatstroke. It might have been a better idea to schedule the Rolling Down the Hill competition for a cooler part of the day.

"Not now," pants Hector, with his eyes still closed.

"Do we have to move?" groans Bru.

"What's a ritual?" says Skooshie, raising his head from the floor to show polite interest – then letting it crash back down because it's too heavy.

Lemur leans forward, his pale face lit with excitement.

"It's a kind of ceremony, a special kind of ceremony."

"Like a wedding?" Skooshie is propped on one elbow now and looking anxious.

"Yes," I say. "It's a leap-year surprise for you. She's a lovely girl, Skooshie. You're going to like being married!"

The look of horror on Skooshie's face is priceless.

A few moments of loud amusement – all at Skooshie's expense – is enough to revive us all.

"Not a wedding, Skoosh," says Lemur, giving him a reassuring thump. Skooshie looks very relieved. "Something important. Maybe the most important thing you have ever done in your life."

We are now all ears.

"Remember the story I told you about how the Lorredan brothers died? And how Christy Lorredan couldn't ever leave this place? Well, I've been thinking about how we could help him."

"Brilliant!" says Skooshie, a bit too enthusiastically.

"What would we do?" asks Bru.

"Well, it doesn't really matter what we do," says Lemur. "It's the fact that we make it up together. It's got to be all of us to make it work. What do you think?"

So we pool what we know about rituals and pick out the bits that sound most fun. Skooshie's well up for it. He liked the words "make it up" and, now we're all pitching in with ideas, seems to feel pretty sure this *is* a game and not a detour into the dark and spooky netherworld.

"Right," says Hector. "So far we've got:

1. Masks
2. Chants
3. Dancing
4. Drums
5. Food."

"Masks," says Bru thoughtfully. "Like Hallowe'en masks?"

"What about making our own?" I say. I dip my fingers in the dust of the den floor and smear it on my cheeks to leave dirty streaks. "That looks good," says Hector.

"The very ground they died on," murmurs Bru. Skooshie, fortunately, doesn't hear this.

"Any suggestions for chants?"

Lemur picks up a stick and looks around. He finds an empty Jaffa Cake box. He starts to hit the stick against the box, settling into a rhythm: *SMACK, tap-tap-tap, SMACK, tap-tap-tap, SMACK, tap-tap-tap*. And he starts to chant, so softly at first that we can't make out what he's saying. The hitting, the chanting get louder, then it's clear: "*TIME to go now! TIME to go now! TIME to go now!*"

We all join in for a bit of a practice, dancing in a circle round the den, until Lemur gets bored and throws down the stick and box. "We'll need better drums obviously," he says.

"Skooshie and I know where we can get drums," says Hector.

"Great. Dancing – I think that'll fall into place once we've got the drums."

"OK. And for the food, everybody just bring something?" says Bru.

"Sounds good," I say. "When are we doing this?"

"Tomorrow," says Lemur. He makes his voice scary. "Tomorrow... at midnight."

"Midnight?" We all stare at him like he's gone mad.

"It'll be scarier if it's dark," he says.

"Yeah, but one small drawback," says Hector. "We'll all be in bed, asleep."

"No way I'll be allowed out at night," says Bru.

"Your mum and dad would let you do that, Lemur?" I ask.

He laughs. "Of course not. I meant let's sneak out."

I don't know what Lemur's house is like, but you'd think he'd've paid a bit of attention when he was in my house or Bru's.

"What do you suggest, that I climb out my bedroom window and dreepy down the wall?" I say. "The only way out of my house is down the hall, right past my mum and dad's bedroom door. If Bru was lying in his own bed at home, with the blankets over his head, my mum could still hear him picking his nose." (Bru looks suitably impressed.) "You think she's not going to hear me unlocking our house door, then opening all the landing doors, then creeping down the stairs?"

"If you can't, you can't," says Lemur with a shrug. "After dinner then?"

"Oh, and Midge," he adds, as we wander down May Terrace on our way home. "Not a word to Kit about this. It's got to be a secret. You don't want to make her curious."

"I wasn't going to tell her," I say. "Why did you think I would tell her?"

"Just don't," he says. "Not this time."

Then he's gone, before I have time to react to the total injustice of being branded the unreliable one.

We'd decided it would be a good idea to get everything in place early so we meet up at the den first thing in the morning.

I've brought a bottle of water.

"Is that all?" asks Bru, looking disappointed. He's been waving a packet of giant marshmallows in my face. I suspect his mum might not yet know that these are missing.

"It's for the masks," I say.

"What??"

I unscrew the top and pour a trickle onto the ground. I scratch up some dust with a stick and mix it to a smooth mud. I stick my finger in this and draw a big dirty line down Bru's nose. "For the masks," I say. He grins. He looks like a crazy, ginger, pint-sized warrior.

"Magic!" he says.

Hector and Skooshie appear with a huge empty tin under each arm. Skooshie is also wearing one on his head. The tins say:

YELLOW CLING PEACHES
Slices in Heavy Syrup

and bring a sticky, sweet smell into the den. There's a sticky, sweet smell about Skooshie for the rest of the day too.

"We got them out the bin behind the Chinese restaurant," Hector explains. "They've always got loads of them."

We wonder if it's possible to attach some kind of strap to the tins, so we can carry them as we dance around. Skooshie has the idea that we could make holes in the bottom and the sides with a tin-opener, then thread string through the holes. But as we don't have a tin-opener or any string, we decide to keep it simple. We find five sticks of more or less the same size. We turn the tins upside down and hit them to test the sound. It's good. We also tear off the cling peaches labelling round each tin, to make them look more spooky ritual and less Chinese restaurant bin.

Finally it's ready. Mudpool prepared (might need topping up with a bit more water later if the day's hot – I leave the bottle beside it). Food piled under one of the drums for safety, and the drum dragged under the shade of the tree for maximum coolness. We've got the marshmallows (brought by Bru), a packet of Hula Hoops (from Skooshie), a poke of big, red raspberries (Lemur), a Curly Wurly (Hector) and a tin of Creamola foam, lemon flavour (that's from me – I've even remembered to bring a spoon to prise open the tin and measure out the crystals fairly and to the correct strength).

All the organising has taken ages.

"What's the time?" Skooshie asks Hector hopefully.

Hector glances at his watch. "Half past nine."

"So we've been here twenty minutes?" I say.

"Could we not just do it now?" asks Bru.

"No!" says Lemur. "It's *got* to be later. It won't work otherwise. We agreed it would be evening."

"OK, OK, keep your knickers on," says Skooshie.

"Well, we're going to have to find *something* to do for the rest of the day," I say.

That's easier said than done. The day passes slowly, slowly, slowly...

We can't settle to anything. We take turns making half-hearted suggestions and turning them down. We loll on the grass and try to play Skooshie's Game but all the things we think of are rubbish. They get so rubbish that thinking up rubbish questions becomes the point of the game. "What'd you choose: to be an octopus or a Mars Bar?" "Have two noses or four ears?" "Be able to fight like a kitten or sing like a kangaroo?"

Which was quite funny.

For a while.

"What are they doing?" says Lemur, standing up and peering down at a load of kids massing between the flats. Kit's in the middle of them.

"Usual wee kid stuff," says Hector.

"Let's go and see," says Lemur. And he's up and off before we can object.

The place is teeming with kids. Really. I don't know where they've all come from. It's like nobody is inside or on holiday – they're all out here.

We approach, interrupting a debate about teams.

"Are you playing rounders?" Lemur asks.

Kit waves the bat she's holding in his direction.

"No, we use this for skipping."

The posse of wee girls surrounding her giggles. The boys in the group marvel at her bravery and lack of respect.

"Let us play."

"Well, I don't know..."

"C'mon. Let us."

"Aw, let them, Kit!" say some of the boys.

And then they're all at it. "Let them, Kit, let them! They're big – it'll be fun."

Lemur steps forward, the kids moving out of his way.

He says something to Kit that we don't hear. She looks at him, her eyes narrowed.

"OK," she says. "But you'll need to do as you're told. Agreed?"

"Agreed."

"What did you say to her?" I ask Lemur as Kit starts organising people into teams.

"That she wasn't very good at rounders. That she wasn't letting us play because she was scared we'd show her up."

He gives an evil grin. And not for the first time, we realise how clever he is.

"HEY, LISTEN!" Kit shouts to get everybody's attention. "Teams: girls against boys!"

Which is met with a roar of approval.

"That was... fun," says Skooshie, much subdued, when we leave the place of battle an hour later.

"Yeah," we agree.

"But never again?"

"Oh, no, never again!"

"Those wee girls were vicious!"

"I was nearly concussed by that one throwing the bat over her shoulder when she started running."

"And look at this bruise on my side – well, it'll be a bruise tomorrow. She wasn't even aiming for base – she threw it *right at me*."

"And such bad winners," says Bru in a shocked tone. "I didn't know wee girls knew words like that..."

24

We've made the den as dark as possible. Everything's in place.

"Anybody for a Creamola foam?" I ask.

The water fizzes as it hits the crystals, bubbling up into a pale yellow froth. We've only got three plastic cups between us, so we have to take turns. The water in the bottle has warmed up in the course of the day and is now the temperature of used bathwater. We sip it appreciatively, hanging onto our turn for as long as possible.

"If you mixed Creamola foam with milk," asks Hector, "would you get a milkshake?"

We think that you probably would. And that it would be worth trying it to find out.

The Curly Wurly proves a nightmare to split fairly. It becomes obvious that we won't be able to bend it into equal parts – that just gets you covered in chocolate and caramel, which leads to arguments about you taking more than your fair share. So we have to trust to honour.

"Take a bite and pass it on," says Hector, passing it to

Lemur first. What he doesn't add but does make clear in his tone is, "And I'm watching you."

We decide to try out the drums. We use Lemur's rhythm first, the Time-to-go-now one.

"It's a bit short," I say.

"And maybe a bit rude?" says Bru. "I mean, he's kind of like a visitor here, and you wouldn't really say that kind of thing to a visitor, would you?"

"Or are we the visitors, if he was here first?" says Hector.

"Yeah, good point, Hector."

"What d'you mean?" asks Skooshie. "This is all to get rid of *him*, isn't it? We're not going to get disappeared?"

It really is hard not to laugh at Skooshie's panic. So we just do.

"Relax, Skooshie," says Lemur. "You'll be fine."

We experiment with different chants. We come up with "*Time, Christy! Time, Christy!*"

"It sounds like we're trying to clear a pub," I say.

And Skooshie comes up with a football-inspired "*Christy Lo-rre-dan! Chri-sty Lo-rre-dan!*" It's definitely one you can get into, it's just like a chant from the terraces.

Then Lemur says, "What about this?" And tapping his drum, he chants quietly,

"*Christy, Christy*
Your time has come."

We agree it's the best so far. We have a bit of a practice getting the rhythm right. Soon we're doing it in unison. If only Mrs Stevenson could see me now, I think. She'd realise what a mistake she made not letting me into the recorder group at school.

"What time is it?" Lemur asks Hector.

"Half past six. Why?"

"Just thinking we should start soon."

"We should do our masks then." There's a drip of water left in the bottle – I had forgotten that we needed it for mud when I was mixing the Creamola foam. I tip it onto the mud pool. There's just enough.

We dip our fingers into the mud and start smearing patterns on our faces. We don't have a mirror so we're relying on each other's reactions to see how well we've managed to do it.

Hector's gone for a lot of clear X shapes, as if his skin has been stitched – he looks like Frankenstein.

Skooshie's approach is to flatten his whole hands into the mud, then clutch his face and forehead to leave giant prints. In fact, there's not much of his skin left visible. He looks really scary until he gives us his big grin.

Bru has used all his fingers at once to cover his face in muddy spots – he looks like he's sufffering from some deadly disease. He's pleased with the looks of disgust we give him.

I've drawn exclamation marks and question marks all over my face. Bru nods approval when he sees it. "You look totally insane," he says.

"Good," I say. "That was the effect I was aiming for."

But Lemur's been the cleverest. He's given himself a curling moustache and small pointy beard and round his eye he's managed (without blinding himself with mud) an eye-patch. It's very dark against his pale face. He looks totally menacing.

"Nice one, Lemur!"

"What's left to eat?" asks Bru.

"The raspberries." Lemur hands them round.

The raspberries are warm too, and sweet and squishy. Red juice runs like blood down our chins when we bite into them.

"Oh, that's the other thing you need for a ritual," says Lemur, with a bloody, raspberry-stained smile. "I forgot to mention it. You need a sacrifice."

Skooshie freezes.

"Like an animal?" I ask, hoping Lemur means insects and not small mammals.

"No!" Lemur laughs. "Like her."

We look in the direction he's pointing. And see Kit standing just inside the entrance to the den.

I'm furious. "*What* are you doing here?" I've got her by the arm.

She shakes herself free and steps further into the den. She spots the empty tin on the ground.

"That's *my* Creamola Foam as well, you know."

"Kit, go home. You're not allowed here. You're not allowed to cross Prospecthill Road."

"*You're* not allowed to go into Cathkin, but you still did it," she says.

"But this is our den – *no one's* allowed here without our invitation."

She looks at me and smiles. "But I was invited."

"*No – you – WEREN'T!*" Four of us at once, loud in outraged protest.

"Lemur invited me."

Lemur isn't denying it. For a moment we're speechless, then we turn on him, tripping over our words because we're so angry.

"You did WHAT? You told ME—"

"What were you THINKING?"

"We've NEVER—"

He stops us by holding up his hand. Maybe it's his pirate disguise. We're not questioning that he's in charge.

"Like I said, every ritual needs a sacrifice."

"It sounds fun," says Kit. "Nice masks, by the way."

This wasn't what we were expecting. But it looks like Lemur has a plan. And Kit seems willing to go along with it. We're waiting to see what happens.

Lemur gives Kit a few raspberries that he'd kept, then makes her stand in the middle. Our drums are positioned around her in a circle.

"Chant," says Lemur.

We follow his start, drumming with our fingers and chanting very softly:

"Christy, Christy

Your time has come."

"Spin," Lemur tells Kit. She starts to birl round in the centre of the circle.

Our drumming gradually gets louder and louder until we're thumping the metal surface hard with our fingers.

"Faster," Lemur tells Kit.

He leaves his drum. We keep drumming and chanting, while Lemur chants and dances in front of us, inside our circle, around Kit. Kit's twirling faster, giggling and breathless.

By now the rhythm of the chant is inside me:

"Your time has come!

Your time has come!"

I don't even hear the words, I'm just part of the

noise. But then there's something wrong, somebody's disrupting the rhythm. It's Lemur. Suddenly I realise he's not singing "Christy, Christy," he's singing, "Kit, Kit."

And then there's a flash, a burst of energy that throws us back from our drums. It shatters the noise. Dazed, we all look at Lemur to explain what has happened. He's standing very still, right in the centre of the den.

And Kit has disappeared.

25

Lemur breathes a sigh of relief. "It worked," he says. He looks pleased with himself, his face flushed with excitement.

"What worked? Where's Kit?" I demand.

Lemur looks surprised. "Haven't you worked it out?"

"WHERE'S KIT?"

"She's gone," he says, as if disappointed he has to spell this out to me. "But I'm here. It means I can stay!"

"Where is she, Lemur? Is she all right?"

"Yes – she's perfectly safe. You don't need to worry about her."

"Why has she disappeared? Why can't I see her?"

Lemur is starting to look a bit concerned about my reaction.

"Kit's not going to be around for a while."

I throw myself at him. He trips, losing his balance and falling onto the cushions. I'm on top of him and punching him as hard as I can and I don't stop until Hector and Skooshie pull me off.

"WHOA, MIDGE – STOP! He's only winding you up."

"No. He isn't." Because I know Lemur and I know that he's telling the truth. "Are you?"

Lemur shakes his head.

"Tell us everything, Lemur," says Bru.

And so he does.

"Do you remember one day in the den we were talking about putting time in a bank?"

"Yes – so you could save it when you didn't need it and use it later."

"And we said we should invent a time bank so we could do that?"

"Yeah..."

"Well, the thing is, I never needed to. Invent it, that is. It's something I can already do."

He looks around us all. "You still don't get it, do you?"

I want to believe that all these days in the sun have scrambled his brains, that what we're listening to is the ravings of somebody with heatstroke. But I know that's not true.

"You're Christy Lorredan," I say.

He grabs me by both arms. "Midge, I knew *you'd* understand."

"Let go of me," I say. "Unless you want me to hit you again."

He backs off.

"I don't get it," says Skooshie.

Lemur punches him.

"Ow!" says Skooshie. "All I said was, 'I don't get it.'"

"You felt that?" says Lemur.

"Yeah, I felt it!" Skooshie's rubbing his arm.

"And you know that you can't feel ghosts, don't you?"

Skooshie's eyes narrow. He suspects some other trick. "I know you're not a ghost, Lemur."

"But Midge is right. I *was* Christy Lorredan. I lived here all those years ago with my mother and father and my brother, Robert."

"And you're here now but not a ghost because you can bank time?" Hector's trying hard to get his head round what's happening here.

"Exactly! The story – I didn't make it up. It all happened the way I told you. Robert dying, then me. But when I died, I was still here. I was stuck – I didn't leave. For some reason I couldn't not be. Do you remember what I told you at the end of the story? That I was waiting and waiting? That's because no one came, no one knew I was here, no one saw me, no one talked to me. Do you know what that feels like?"

"It would be bad," Bru admits.

"Imagine it. Imagine how much you would long for someone to play with. And this went on and on – I don't know for how long. The house was a ruin. No one ever came into the grounds. It had all grown wild. Then one day I heard something. I was in the tree where the tree house had been – it was long gone too. I saw someone in the undergrowth. A boy. I watched him squeezing through the brambles, eventually finding the open space beneath my tree. He sat down and leaned against the trunk. He opened a bag and took out some bread and cheese and ate them. Then he lay down on the ground and fell asleep."

Lemur pauses here. He swallows hard.

"At last here was someone to talk to. I knew he was

tired so I let him sleep, waiting until it looked like he was going to wake up. What was a few more hours to wait after all that time? I climbed down from my tree and went up to him. The place he had picked to rest was exactly where Robert fell. Where I fell. I remember hoping it hadn't given him bad dreams.

"He must have heard me because he jumped up, really alarmed, and all set to run away.

"'It's all right,' I said, reaching out to him to reassure him. I couldn't believe he was actually able to see me! The last thing I wanted was for him to leave. 'I'm Christy,' I said. 'Please – stay! You can't go!'

"When my hand touched his arm, there was a flash, like an explosion. I covered my eyes because it was so bright it hurt. When I looked again, the boy was gone. I collapsed on the grass, and I cried and cried. I realised the whole thing must have been a dream.

"But when the sun came up in the morning I saw it. The boy's bag. I hadn't dreamt it at all. I rummaged through it. An end of bread. A piece of cheese. A book. A book with a name in it: Stuart Coulter.

"And then I realised that I felt different. I had so much energy. It was a strange feeling, but a fantastic one. And even more strange: I was hungry. I ripped off a hunk of bread. I broke the cheese into pieces and stuffed them in my mouth. They were the best things I had ever tasted. Does that seem odd to you? It won't if you think about it. *I had eaten nothing since I died.*"

"So you were alive again?" says Hector.

"Yes."

"Because you stole that boy's life," I say. "Stuart

Coulter – he was dead. And now you've murdered my sister."

"No," says Lemur. "He was *not dead*! And I haven't killed Kit either. I met him again. Honestly, I did. Look, I didn't know how it had happened. But it was a chance for me and I had to take it. I found friends. I had people to play with and talk to again."

"And you got this from Stuart Coulter. How can that work? What did you take?"

"What was Stuart Coulter like when you saw him again?"

Lemur looks at the ground. "An old man," he says.

"He took his *time*," says Hector.

"He's a time thief," I say.

Even Skooshie's got it by now. He's not impressed.

"So you nick time from people?" he says. "They go straight from being children to being old. And you use the time in between."

Lemur nods.

"What happens when you've used up one person's time?"

"I need to find someone else."

"Like Kit."

"Yes, like Kit." He looks at me defiantly. "Why not Kit? I chose her for *you*. You're always going on about how annoying she is."

"We all go on about how annoying our brothers and sisters are! It doesn't mean I said it was OK to make her disappear! Why did you pick on her?"

"It had to be someone who would come here and take part willingly. It had to happen here – like I told you. The ritual didn't matter – we could have done anything. I just needed to have someone here – with me right on the spot where I died. And I couldn't sacrifice any of you. So I persuaded Kit to come – it wasn't hard. I knew she wouldn't be able to resist being part of the gang."

He means every word of this. And Kit's gone.

"So you've kept going all that time and now you're..." Hector does a quick calculation in his head, " ...168?"

"No," says Lemur. "I'm still twelve."

"You're still twelve," I repeat. "And you'll never get any older?"

"That's right."

"So even though you make friends, you lose them all the time, because they grow up and you don't."

He nods, looking miserable for a minute.

"That's going to happen again with us, you know, Lemur," says Bru. "We're going to get older."

"No! You're different. You're the first people I've trusted enough to tell. I'm Lemur not Christy any more – you gave me that name! We can work out how to stay together. So that nothing ever changes. You can be like me! We'd never get any older, any of us – it would always be like this!"

No one knows what to say to this. Our silence throws Lemur.

"OK," he says. "OK. The game's a bogey, as Skooshie would say. I'll bring Kit back and we'll start again. With someone else. You'll help me. C'mon."

It's Hector who says what everyone's thinking. "We're not going to help you do this, Lemur. It's not right."

"What kind of friends are you? I'd do it for you! Don't we always stick together?

"None of us would ask you to do something like this," says Bru. "Like Hector says, it's just not right."

"Well, I don't need your help! Do you know that boy wasn't missed when I used up his life? Nor were any of the others. Because that's the clever thing. I take people and life just closes up around them. No one remembers they were ever born. No one misses them. That boy's mother woke up the next day with no thought of him in her head. No one remembered me and now no one remembers them. Isn't that funny? What happened to me, I can make happen to other people now."

"You can't tell us what to think!" I shout back.

"Oh, yes, I think you'll find that I can, Midge. And when it happens, you'll have no memory of Kit or any of this."

"Why did you bother telling us then?" asks Bru. "Why not just make it happen so we don't know? We just forget and everything goes on as normal?"

"Because I wanted you to know the whole story. I wanted you to understand what I need to do."

"You want this to be our fault, not just yours." It sounds like Skooshie speaks from bitter experience, like he's very familiar with this approach of shared blame.

"Whatever happens now, you'll share the responsbility. I can bring Kit back and we'll find someone else – and you'll remember everything that happens. Or, if it's easier for you, I can make you forget and Kit will be gone. What are you going to choose?"

He makes it sound like Skooshie's Game, like we have no option but to choose. That's the rules. I have two thoughts. (1) I have to help Kit. (2) I really want to hit Lemur again.

I catch Hector's eye. He puts his hand on my arm, either to stop me flying at Lemur or to reassure me, maybe both.

"Kit back. Then we'll help you," he says to Lemur. "You're right. We need to stick together."

Lemur grins. "You mean it? What about the rest of you?" he asks.

I nod. "Yes," I say, maybe a bit too quickly.

"Me too," says Bru.

"And me," says Skooshie. He shoots his arm out, waiting for the rest of us to clap our hands on top of his.

But then the smile on Lemur's flushed face fades.

"Do you think I don't know that you're lying? All you want to do is help Midge save Kit. You have no intention of helping me... I thought we would do anything for each other."

Bru and Skooshie look at their feet. I can only glower at Lemur while Hector tries to convince him that we mean what we say. He's not convincing anybody.

Lemur storms out of the den.

"What do we do now?" says Bru.

"We don't panic," says Hector firmly. "If we just stick together, we're stronger than Lemur. He can't make us forget."

He can't, can he?

26

When I wake up, I lie in bed, thinking about the night before. It was a long telling off. I think, not for the first time, that it must be quite good to be Skooshie – there are so many of them, his parents don't really notice if he stays out a bit late. But my parents can concentrate all their attention on me – they're always on my case. On the plus side, I don't have to share a bedroom with three brothers, like Skooshie does. It is nice to have a room all to yourself.

My mum crashes in looking for clothes to wash. She picks things up from the floor and the chair, wrinkling her nose in disgust.

"You've been wearing these shorts for days. They can practically stand up on their own, they're that dirty. I'm not going into the pockets – here, you clear them out."

I wait until she's gone before I sort through my stuff. There's an unexpected treat there – a sherbet dip. Those don't usually make it to the next day but perfect for breakfast! Yeah – I bought it at the garage on the way home last night – that made me even later getting back. I frown because there's something nagging at the back of my mind. What was it the man at the garage said? He was surprised. "A pen? Do you want me to gift-wrap it for you as well?"

Why had I wanted a pen? What was it for? I turn the sherbet dip round and that's when I notice the big black letters written on the back.

I bump into Bru – literally – as I sprint out of our flats to go and find him.

"Hiya," he says. "Is it today we're going to the park? I've got some money – maybe we could scrape together enough between us for a round of pitch and putt?"

"C'mon," I say. "We need to get to the den."

The others are deep in conversation when we get there.

"Hey!" calls Lemur. "What took you so long? We're just wondering if it would be possible to get into Queen's Park after dark? Or we could hang about in the bushes as it gets dark and get ourselves locked in!" He's loud and jumping about the place. There's something odd about it, like he's had too much sugar or he's trying too hard.

"I've got a sister," I say, interrupting him. "Her name's Kit. She's two years younger than me. She's small, with brown hair, quite annoying."

"Midge, if you're going to have an imaginary family member, go for a brother. An older brother – much better than a sister. That'd be a real pain."

"I do have a sister, Hector. She calls you 'the Inspector' and Skooshie 'Stookie'. She calls Bru 'Bru' – I think she likes him. She doesn't like Lemur – she's always been a bit suspicious of him. And she was right to be."

"What?" says Lemur. "Are you feeling all right, Midge? Has the heat got to your head?"

"*Think.*" I am looking at them – Bru, Hector, Skooshie. I am trying hard not to shout. "Please think. D'you not remember when she was about five and she decided to leave home and she was heading off with her wee bag packed but the van arrived so she decided to stay, just till the next day?"

"Pal," Bru has his arm round my shoulder, trying to calm me down. "We're just not finding it that funny." I shake him off furiously.

"Kit, Kit, Kit – short for Kirsty. She decided she needed a nickname because we all had one. You suggested 'Krusty', Skooshie, and she hit you. You must remember!"

Still blank expressions on their faces.

"Or the time she spent all the money for my birthday present on herself? She bought a big box of chocolates, which she kept. And the only thing she got me was..."

"**A SHERBET DIP!**" Hector and Bru yell at the same time as I wave the packet in front of them.

"YES!" I thrust the sherbet in Lemur's direction. It's like we're in court and I'm producing the final bit of evidence that shows what a liar he is.

"Do you remember what Lemur said to us? That we'd forget it all. I bought this last night on the way home – I can't see one without thinking of Kit. And I wrote on the back. Look."

I hold it out. In big accusing letters:

SAVE KIT – LEMUR LIES.

Lemur looks at me with a kind of grudging respect. Then he says, "Actually I've never lied to you. You're my friends. I just didn't tell you the whole truth till now."

He sits down on the cushions, slumps against the tree. "If I get you Kit back, I won't have long. Can't you see that? Didn't you see how tired and pale I got before the ritual? I'd run out of time. But look at me now – I'm just like you. I need to do it. It's the only way."

Skooshie goes to sit down on one of the drums on the other side of the den. He stops himself, then steps back. It's clear he means to give the middle of the den a very wide berth.

"It's all right, Skoosh," says Lemur. "Nothing's going to happen to you."

"I just thought – you know – we've been standing on the spot for months and we could've disappeared at any time?"

"No. I need to make it happen. It only works when I decide to take your time."

"Nick," I say. "Not take. Don't try and pretend it's not wrong."

"Is it wrong?" says Lemur. "It doesn't hurt them."

I'm looking at him and I'm wondering where Lemur went. The old Lemur, the one who captained us to our famous footballing victory at the recs, who jumped up and down with delight when he watched *The Flashing Blade*, who helped us get revenge on Mrs Whistle-Blower for Bru, who planked a ball in Cathkin so we could play on the pitch. It doesn't feel like he's here any more either.

You see, what I can't get out of my head is all the lost stories. Stuart Coulter's, Kit's. The others' – how many others? The things they were going to do. The things that would have happened to them. The people they were going to be.

Lemur's not seeing any of that. He asked us to imagine what it was like for him but I don't think he has at any time imagined what it was like for those other children. He needs to.

"He'd run away from home," I say.

"Who had?" They're all confused at this turn in the conversation.

"Stuart Coulter. He'd run away from home. The book in his bag was the only thing he was able to take with him – that and some food, just enough to keep him going for a couple of days."

Lemur starts to interrupt but I just make my voice louder.

"Life at home was really tough, unbearable, since his mother had married again. His stepfather used to hit him. So he decided he'd go and find his dad's brother, who lived in the Borders. He could stay there. He'd been walking for a long time and he needed somewhere to sleep and he thought the overgrown park was the perfect place. He'd be safe there. He kept patting his bag to make sure the book was in there. It had been a present from his dad. His dad had written Stuart's name—"

"*THAT'S – NOT – TRUE!*" Lemur roars.

"Isn't it?" I say. "How do you know? The fact is, Lemur, that he had a life and he had a story that you nicked from him. You never gave him the chance to tell you!"

"I didn't do it on purpose!"

"Not the first time," I say. "But after that you did. I bet there was a wee girl! What about the wee girl?"

"No—"

"Did you even know all their names? Yes, because you would have become friends with them, just friendly enough to suggest exploring the deserted park together. Just enough to get them in here. So, the wee girl. I'm guessing she was called – Mary. She really trusted you. Or maybe she felt sorry for you—"

Lemur has his hands over his ears now. He's yelling at me to stop.

"I'll shut up if you tell us about them."

"I don't know about—

"Yes, *Mary* felt sorry for you. She had a big family and she could see that you— "

"Stop. Please... stop. I'll tell you."

"No lies. And no half-truths. And nothing missed out, Lemur."

"I'll tell you everything."

Lemur takes a deep breath, as if to steady himself.

"You're right I didn't know anything about Stuart Coulter. When I met him again – and this was more than thirty years after that day he fell asleep at the bottom of the tree – there was something in his eyes that made me think he knew I was somehow important to him. But he couldn't work out how. He'd only caught a glimpse of me, remember? But I knew it was him. It was like he had found me, even after all that time.

"I didn't want to know anything about him. I kept my distance and I watched. And as I watched I started to feel different."

"How?"

"Weaker, slower, paler. I remembered that empty feeling. I didn't want to go back there."

"How long did that last?

"Until I found someone else."

"Whose time did you steal next?

"His name was Eric Gemmell. His father had a stall in the market. We came into the park to collect blackberries to sell." Lemur pauses. "He was a fast runner, faster even than you, Bru. He had a dog, a scruffy little terrier called Patch. It followed me around for months afterwards.

"And yes, there was a girl. Her name was Sarah – I never found out her surname. By that time they had cleared some of the park and built on the land. Only the space in between was safe, my den. Sarah lived in one of the big houses on May Terrace. She was exploring when she found me, lying here weak and totally out of time. She liked stories – I told her all about Mount Lorredan Hall. If it hadn't been too late for me I would have let her go. I think we would have become friends...

"She found me later too. I met her, forty, fifty years afterwards. The same pale hair, the same blue eyes."

"Did she still think you were fun, Lemur?" I ask. "Was she still asking you to tell her stories?"

He ignores me. "They kept finding me. It always warned me that I was running out of time."

"And what about them? How much time have they got after they see you again?"

I don't need an answer. I know where Kit is and what's happening to her. She's not anywhere. She's waiting – waiting like those other children waited. She'll have plenty of time to wonder if I was part of it, if I said it was OK to use her and helped Lemur make it happen. She's waiting for the moment when she will reappear, in a time she doesn't know, among people she doesn't recognise. Until one day she will see Lemur again. And the only consolation he'll give her is that, although her new life is confusing and scary, it won't be a very long one.

27

"And after her," says Hector, "it was Mr Murphy."

There's an "Oh..." from Skooshie, as he catches up and the last pieces fall into place for him. "So that's why he tried to strangle you. That's why he called you a thief!"

"And that's why he told me to watch out for Lemur! He wasn't telling me to look after him – it was a warning."

"Joe Murphy was my friend," says Lemur emphatically. "I went to see him when he asked me to."

"When did you see him?" asks Hector.

"The day Midge saw me and waited for me, because he thought I was coming for him."

"When we said Midge was imagining things?"

"Yes."

"And I said he needed glasses?" Skooshie appears more outraged at having been misled in this than by anything else so far.

"You really went?"

"Yes, Hector, I really went!" Lemur sighs. "I realised I was being a coward, avoiding him."

He looks quickly round us, maybe hoping somebody

will say, "Hey, Lemur, that was really brave of you." We don't. We're waiting to hear what happened.

"Well?" I say when Lemur doesn't speak. "What did Joe Murphy really say to you when you went to see him?"

"He talked about Third Lanark."

"The football team?"

"No, Skooshie, Third Lanark the famous brand of ginger. Now shut up and let Lemur talk."

"Joe was a big Third Lanark fan. That's where I first saw him – coming out of the park with his dad. He talked about them all the time."

"So when was this?"

"Some time in the 1920s."

Skooshie looks as though he's about to raise an objection but Bru dunts him in the ribs with his elbow.

"He talked about the last match he'd seen. His favourite player, Anderson, had scored. He described the goal blow by blow. All the passes that led up to it – he remembered every one."

"You told us about that match," Bru interrupted, earning a glare from Skooshie. "You described it to us."

"Yes. I got that from Joe. I wasn't able to get inside the ground. It's funny. Though I've been around since Cathkin was just a field and I saw the stand and the terraces being built and the park being laid out, I had never been inside until we went. Going there with you was the most special thing I've ever done."

We look at each other. Cathkin. Just one of the many things that glue us together.

"Joe – Mr Murphy – told me when I went to his flat

that he could still feel how cold it had been standing on the terraces, that he remembered stamping his feet to try and keep warm. It had been so cold that he'd wrapped his football scarf three times around his head covering his mouth – but he'd had to push it down because he couldn't cheer properly. That he could still taste the bar of chocolate that his mother had given him to eat at half time. That he still heard the noise of the fans' football rattles in his dreams.

"Then he reminded me about how he'd come straight to see me after the game, to tell me about it.

"Look." He fishes a scrap of pink paper out of his pocket, unfolds it and holds it out to us.

It's a ticket for a football match. **THE THIRD LANARK ATHLETIC CLUB** stands out at the top, and further down the words **Saturday, 10 November, 1923**. It's in surprisingly good condition.

"That's his ticket. He still had it when I went to see him."

"So how do you have it now?"

"He made me take it. So that I wouldn't forget what I'd done. Ever."

Lemur puts the ticket back in his pocket and continues. "Joe was so excited that day. Not just about the game but also because he'd found out he was going away. His family were emigrating to America.

"'But you won't go?' I said. I couldn't bear the thought of being on my own again. I was so close to telling Joe everything.

"He said, 'Of course I'm going! Have you any idea what opportunities I'll have there? I'll miss you, of course, Christy, I will. Maybe you can come and visit me some time.'

"I don't know if he meant it. I only knew that there was no possibility that I could ever leave here. Away from my den, I would have nowhere to hide and no way to keep going.

"So now it was too late to tell Joe. I didn't have time to persuade him to stay, let alone explain how I needed his help. And he was so keen to go. He didn't care that he was leaving me. That made me angry with him."

"So he was the next one?"

"Yes... I didn't need to do it. I had time left over. I could have waited a while but I didn't. I took his time there and then. And his parents went off to America not even remembering they'd ever had a son."

Lemur looks directly at me for the first time. "I missed Joe. He was a lot of fun. You wouldn't believe how much he loved football. But hopeless at playing – two left feet. Worse than me even, Midge."

"He must've been bad," I say with half a smile, though I try not to.

"Then he reappeared here at the end," says Lemur gloomily. "Like they always do. They find me, just before they die."

"Why did he want to see you?" asked Hector.

"He wanted Lemur to change things back," says Bru before Lemur can answer.

"Yes," says Lemur. "He wanted to be twelve again."

"But you couldn't do it?" I ask.

"Not by then. It was too late. I had used up all his time."

"Did you tell him that?"

"No. But I think he knew."

Oh, he knew all right. I think about Mr Murphy crying and now I know why.

"And that's what will happen to Kit?" asks Bru. "Some day in about sixty years' time you'll bump into her. She'll be an old lady but you'll look exactly the same. She'll know who you are, she'll remember what happened. She'll remember Midge, and Hector and Skoosh and me as well, but she won't know us any more. She'll be all on her own, with no story and hardly any time left."

"But I can't let go," says Lemur. He looks like he's about to start crying. "I can't. I want to stay here. I want to stay with you."

"It isn't fair, Lemur," I say. "Can you see Hector doing this? D'you think Bru would do it? Or Skooshie?"

He looks at me. This time he's not avoiding the questions.

"No," he says.

"It's not your turn any more, Lemur."

28

You know by now that we are really good at not talking about stuff we don't want to discuss. Well, that day, as my dad would say, we surpass ourselves. No one would have guessed that it was Lemur's last day. It could have been any day in that long, hot summer.

We follow the route marched by Mary's army up and over Prospecthill Road, making appropriate military sound effects along the way. In the recs we go into action. The five of us charge forward with fearsome battle cries so scary that the (totally invisible) forces against us scatter in confusion and we win the day.

Once inside the park gates, we split up for the scavy hunt: Bru, Hector and Skooshie in one team; me and Lemur in the other. The goal is the flagpole. But on the way you have to collect stuff. Today these are: a pine cone, an ice-lolly stick, an orange handprint.

"An actual print," says Hector. "You can't just turn up with an orange hand."

Apart from that there are no rules. Winners are the first team with all the items to touch the flagpole.

Bru, Hector and Skoosh set off at a run, straight up the hill. But Lemur and I pause to discuss tactics.

"OK," I say. "There's only one set of tennis courts between here and the flagpole so that's where we need to get the dust for the handprint. It's near here so we should do it first."

"Agree."

"But first we need a bit of paper to do the handprint on. That must be what they've gone to look for."

"Disagree," says Lemur. And he's off and running. "C'MON!"

The tennis courts are made of the same dusty orange stuff as the pitches in the recs. So it's easy enough to get a handprint. The tricky part is getting onto the courts. You have to get by the man in the booth. He's really only interested in letting people who want to play tennis onto the courts. People who can pay.

"Talk to him, Midge," says Lemur.

"Good morning," I say, planting my elbows on the booth.

He is instantly suspicious. "Yeah?"

"I was wondering," (I'm aware of Lemur at the height of my ankles trying to sneak in unnoticed), "if you would perhaps be good enough to tell me the actual cost in money for me and some friends – some very good friends of mine – to play on these lovely courts."

"Look, son, do you actually have any money or are you just wasting my time?"

"How could it be a waste of time when it's a lovely sunny day and we're having this nice conversation?" I realise I may have gone too far because he's got up out of his seat now and he's looking annoyed. Then Lemur pops up beside me.

"Got it!"

"Thanks, mister!" I say and we run off. The man throws a few swear words after us but it's half-hearted. It's too hot for him to really care.

"So where do we get the paper for the handprint?" I ask.

"We don't," says Lemur. "Stand still."

He clamps his left hand to my back, then pushes my chest really hard with his right hand. "See?"

The print is bold and clear against my (once) white t-shirt. I look down admiringly. "I quite like that. I might keep it."

"Pine cone next."

We spread out among the trees, looking hard. We wander along towards the gate at Victoria Road, then up the hill again, so we don't get too far from the flagpole. We're having no luck.

"It would help if we knew what a pine tree looked like," grumbles Lemur.

"There!" I whisper.

"Where?" He's looking for a tree but I've spotted something more useful. Hector bending down to pick up something from the ground. "Hector's found one. There'll be more round there."

We wait until Hector's moved away so he doesn't see us. When we get to the patch of trees, we realise he's tried to hide the other pine cones by kicking them into the bushes.

"Nice try, Hector," I say. "But not quite smart enough to out-fox us."

"Only the ice-lolly stick now," says Lemur.

"Ice-lolly stick, ice-lolly stick..." We're scanning the ground, but it's a big park. There are plenty of sticks, but none of the lolly variety to be seen.

"Wee kids!" I say with sudden inspiration.

We start running towards the swings. And there is a wee kid there, halfway through a bright-red ice lolly. It's melting faster than he can eat it, and there's red stuff running down his arm.

"Hey," I say. "Can we have your lolly stick when you're done?"

He looks up at us and his lip starts to quiver. "Mu-u-um!"

"No, no! I don't want your lolly, honest! Just the stick." Now his mum's arrived and she's looking really unimpressed. "I wasn't trying to take his lolly," I say. "We're playing this game and I just need a lolly stick—"

"MIDGE!" Lemur's standing by the bin at side of the swing park. Well, not so much standing by it as half in it while he rummages through the contents. What a piece of brilliance!

I run over to him, shouting over my shoulder to the wee kid, "SORRY! ENJOY YOUR LOLLY!"

I'm asking, "Any luck?" when Lemur turns to me, triumphantly waving a lolly stick. The wee kid's mum is looking at us with a disgusted expression on her face.

"That's it. Let's go!"

The flagpole's in sight. We're heading for it full pelt when we see Bru sprinting in from the side. He's really legging it.

"RUN!"

We're a bit nearer than Bru but he's not giving up. We throw ourselves over the fencing and lunge at the pole. Bru touches it at exactly the same time we do.

"WE WON!" I shout, as Hector and Skooshie jog into view a few seconds later.

"Draw!" protests Bru.

"No – our whole team was here first! Yours has only just arrived."

We look at Hector. He usually has the last word on rules.

"Aw, we didn't think of that," he says.

We don't have enough money for the boats, but we sit on the swings by the boating pond and call out warnings, telling the people rowing and paddling to watch out for the dead soldiers lurking under the water.

"Whoah!" shouts Lemur as two boats collide. "Did you see that?"

"Those two hands reaching up out of the water?" says Bru.

"Yeah – they shoved that boat into the other one!"

"WATCH OUT, MRS!" Skooshie shouts to a woman lying back in her boat, with her hand trailing in the water. "They'll pull you over the side!" Unfortunately for her, she's too far away to hear him.

We're hoping for a sinking (very rare) or at least some daredevil ending up in the water (less rare), but today's not the day for it. So we move on.

Between us we manage to scrape together enough

money for two pokes of chips. We run up Victoria Road, with the chips wrapped in Hector's t-shirt to keep them hot. We're planning to get to the stones before we eat them but with the first waft of vinegar and hot chips, everybody agrees that's a rubbish plan, and we drop onto the first bench we come to and eat them there. And then we wander up to the stones, the highest part of the park. There's not much to do there but we always go. It's in an area that's wilder. The grass is allowed to grow long and there are dirt pathways, not tarmac. There are no flowers or neatly cut bushes – it all feels a bit neglected. It's that and the remoteness and the view of the city that we like, I think. The stones look quite important but we don't really wonder why they're there. We just know you get a better view when you stand on them. And that it's fun jumping from one to another.

When we've exhausted the park – and the park has exhausted us – we head for home. I tell my mum Lemur's parents have had to go out and is it all right if he has dinner with us?

"Of course," she says. "Come on in, Lemur." And my dad grins at him and says, like he always does, "Anytime – it's just a few more potatoes in the pot."

Lemur sits in Kit's place because of course she's not here.

We're just about to leave my house and go and find the others. I'm showing Lemur the postcards I got at the art gallery.

He says, "Here." And he presses into my hand a pink slip of paper. Joe Murphy's ticket. "So you don't forget."

"We'll never forget you, Lemur! How could we? You've been a totally memorable pain in the arse."

That makes him laugh. Luckily. "And so have you," he says, giving me a thump. "Don't let Kit get her hands on it. She's always taking your stuff."

"I won't."

Though it's evening, it's still really hot. "D'you know what I'm thinking?" says Bru. "That this is perfect weather for a water fight."

We use old washing-up liquid bottles. You can squirt a long way with them. "Not in the eyes," my mum always says firmly. "I've washed them out but if you get a bit of Fairy in your eye it'll really hurt." We don't listen. It does nip a bit, but if you're stupid enough to get caught full in the face, then that's your lookout.

It's Bru and me against Hector and Lemur. Skooshie's a free agent, floating between the teams, sometimes on our side and sometimes against us. It mainly results in him getting soaked by us all.

We refill the bottles using the tap down by the lock-ups that's meant for people washing their cars. Hector considers whether we should have rules on how many times you're allowed to refill and whether you're allowed to defend the tap to stop the other team refilling. He stops talking when we all squirt him at once. "OK. A free-for-all it is," he says.

And then the water fight begins. And we take some hits but we give as good as we get. Whoever planned these flats was dead clever. So many walls to duck behind and nooks to dive into and opportunities for ambush – obviously someone who had enjoyed a water fight or two in his childhood.

"Ready?" mouths Bru.

"Ready," I mouth back.

Lemur, Hector and Skooshie are pressed against the lock-up wall, planning to sneak up to the corner, then leap out and get us. What they don't know is that Bru and I aren't around the corner. We've climbed onto the lock-up roof. We've crept to the edge on our bellies. We are right above them.

"NOW!" I yell.

That makes them look up. And we get all three of them right in the face.

It is without doubt our most glorious moment.

We're lying in the long grass, exhausted and soaking wet. Skooshie is wringing the front of his t-shirt and we're laughing at the long stream of water that runs out. The front door of the flats trundles open, announcing my dad on his way to work. Time's almost up. He struggles to pick us out in the fading light. I wave down to him. "We're just walking them up the road, then I'll go up."

"OK, son. See you in the morning."

We get up to go, reluctant to let the evening slip away

from our grasp. We must all be tired because we make slow progress going up the hill.

"Great fight," says Lemur.

"Pure dead brilliant," says Hector.

"A shame you lost," says Bru.

"We didn't lose!" says Skooshie.

"Oh, I think you did!" I say.

Skooshie grins. "Next time," he says. "Just wait till next time."

It's Bru who starts to sing first. We all join in. We sing it as we walk, not loudly like we usually do, like we're François challenging the Spanish, but quietly, like we're determined and deadly serious. And we walk even more slowly so that we've time to finish it before we get to the road.

"Let's always take whatever comes
And never try to hide.
Face everything and anyone
Together side by side."

Hector and Skooshie stay on our side while Lemur crosses Prospecthill Road. It's the last we see of him. Lemur, walking backwards and waving. Just before he's lost in the trees and the dark, he cups his hands to his mouth and yells. *"See youse later. See youse."*

29

We're in the den, the four of us. We know it will be the last time. Outside it's hot, but the den is cool and shady.

I've managed to sneak four mugs out of the house, plus some Irn-Bru that my dad had planked in a cupboard for the next time he has a bottle of whisky. I was nearly caught red-handed (or ginger-handed, even) but Kit had worked out what I was up to and distracted him long enough for me to get it out of the house. So now I owe her. I wonder what her price will be?

They hold out the mugs and I pour the ginger into each one.

"To Lemur. Who we will never forget." We clatter the mugs together in a toast, then drink.

"And to us," says Hector. "Who will never part." A second clattering.

We pull back the vegetation growing over the hollow at the back of the tree. We don't break it off, just prop it back so we can get to the trunk.

And beneath the carved writing that's already there, Hector uses his dad's penknife to add:

LEMUR
MISSED BY
MIDGE, BRU, HECTOR, SKOOSHIE

"Add **TOGETHER SIDE BY SIDE**," says Skooshie. "He was a big *Flashing Blade* fan."

"Yeah?" asks Hector.

"Yeah." We all think it's a good idea.

It takes a while. Skooshie offers to help out, but to be honest his spelling can be a bit dodgy.

And before letting the green stuff spring back into place, we tuck into the hollow: an empty washing-up bottle we used in the water fight, a piece of souvenir concrete from Cathkin, and Bru's football – the one we'd used at the recs.

"Are you sure, Bru?" Hector asks.

Bru nods and Skooshie takes his foot away from the branches he's been holding back. The hollow disappears from sight once again.

Then it's time to leave. We pile up sticks and leaves and stones behind us, to block the entrance to the den. It's not that we think it's unsafe – it's just that we don't want anybody else to go there because it was ours.

We go and sit in the grass at the top of the hill. It must be nearly time for them to cut it again. When you lie down, it's so long it tickles your nose.

We're quiet for a while. I guess we're all thinking about Lemur and how we're going to miss him. Then

Skooshie's belly makes a noise a bit like a cat singing along to a badly played violin. And, weirdly, that helps.

Bru's playing with a ladybird, moving it from stalk to stalk in his hands. "It's funny," he says, "how your interests change as you get older."

"What do you mean?"

"Well, for example, we haven't talked about the bins in ages."

"Aw, the bins," says Hector.

It's true. It started as a conversation about stuff we were afraid of. Places you can't just walk by – you have to run. You don't know for definite that there's anything scary there but you have your suspicions... And I was telling them that for Kit, it's the place where the bins are.

When you live in flats like ours, you don't take your rubbish outside. Each floor has a rubbish chute. You pull open the heavy metal front – it opens in a V. You up-end your kitchen bin into it (taking care not to put in anything too bulky), then close the front. The whole load of rubbish is tipped into nothingness, falling floors and floors into the huge bins down on the ground. It's worth lingering to hear the noise it makes as it plunges down, especially from six floors up. It's also worth sorting through a bin a bit (avoiding the muckier stuff) and selecting items to send down on their own, just to hear what they sound like. An empty bean can is a favourite of mine (you flip the flap closed quickly to try and make it bounce off the chute walls as it goes down – it makes a brilliant plingy noise) or something heavy, like a pair of old shoes (you wait, wait, wait, and then there's a dull but very satisfying thud that echoes up from the bottom).

Sometimes I used to hang about holding the chute flap open a crack, to watch for stuff from floor 7 shooting by. A draft of cold air hits you in the face, a distant pong of rubbish, always with a waft of old bananas. But I've never managed to see any. Bru and I worked out that I was unlikely to, as I was depending on only six families emptying their bins while I was waiting. Whereas, if we waited further down, there were six families using the chute on *each of the floors* above us, so more chance of catching sight of their rubbish. So we took to hanging about on floors where we'd no business to be, checking out the chute. When this didn't work, we decided we needed to take a more scientifically active role. If a bin needed emptying, one of us stood ready, while the other raced downstairs a few floors to glimpse the contents shooting by. It could have developed into a brilliant game, with the glimpser trying to identify and remember all the items falling past him. We took it in turns to chuck and to observe, but it was a short-lived experiment. People objected to us hanging about their chutes, with or without bins, and chased us with a threat to tell our mothers.

Now I come to think about it, I might have been the one who started Kit's bin worries. Yeah, it might have been me. Though I was only joking when I used to threaten to put her down the chute. I only did it when she really annoyed me. "Head first, Kit. But don't worry – the rubbish will be nice and soft for landing on. A bit smelly, but nice and soft."

She'd squeal, "No, no no no – don't let him, Mum, don't let him!" That's when she was really wee. Later on she just looked at me as if she'd like to see me try. Sadly, she's too big now. She'd only block it. And that wouldn't be fair on the neighbours.

You can't see the bins at the bottom of the chute. They're under the ground-floor flats, shut away behind a brown double door with vents high up. The lift machinery's in there too.

"Well, it *might* be the lift that makes the strange noises," Skooshie said. "Or it might be something else..."

No one ever goes in there – except the caretaker, I suppose, to check the level of rubbish in the bin and move a new one into place. And the bin men, of course, to empty the bins. The topic of the bins used to keep us busy. There was a lot to think about.

Questions we asked: Why do we never see the caretaker going in there? Why does the bin motor come so early in the morning that we miss it too? Why have we never seen the door open, never seen inside?

"For all we know," said Bru, "it isn't bins in there at all – there is in fact a huge, rubbish-devouring monster lurking in the dark."

Hector nodded his agreement. "So whenever somebody opens the chute, it sees the light and opens its mouth to eat what comes down."

"Yeah. And as long as we keep feeding it by chucking stuff down the chutes, it stays there."

"If we stopped," said Lemur, "it would burst through the brown double door with a single flick of its long scaly tail and go on the rampage."

"**THONK, THONK, THONK!**" Skooshie's imitation of the monster, crushing all in its path, was pretty impressive, as I remember. "It would go for the oldsters first. They're slow-moving and easy to catch."

I could see that happening. "Yeah, it would knock them out by belching deadly rubbish fumes in their faces."

So I was an oldster, the prey of the rubbish monster, and as Skooshie breathed noisily on me, I went rigid, then keeled over.

"We'll have to try and trick it back into the bin place!" shouted Hector, coming to the rescue.

"What about a trail of really tasty rubbish?" Bru called to him.

"Good one!"

"Or we could offer ourselves as bait," said Lemur, "then nip out once we'd got it back inside."

"That's a plan! Let's do it!"

And that's what we did. And I was saved – and the flats were saved! And probably the rest of the world as well. Not that anybody round here's ever expressed their gratitude either in words or in small presents.

"I suppose every block of flats has its own rubbish monster, Midge?" said Bru, when the monster was once again in captivity and order was restored. As Bru and I are the ones that actually live in the flats, above the rubbish monster's lair, it was accepted that we were the experts on rubbish monster behaviour.

"I would think so."

And Bru puffed the air out of his cheeks, thinking the unthinkable. "Wow. Better hope they never plan an outbreak together."

We laugh. It's still funny, even now, though we're older and we've moved on.

"It doesn't matter about the bins," I say.

"I wasn't saying it did," says Bru. "I don't need to keep talking about the bins."

"No, I mean it doesn't matter that we don't talk about the bins *any more*. What matters is that we *used to talk* about the bins. That there was a time when you and me and Skooshie and Hector and Lemur shared a conversation about the bins. D'you know what I mean?"

"Yes," says Bru. "Of course I do."

And as we sit in the grass, I realise I'm not worried about school. I'm not scared of losing them – Skoosh, Hector and Bru and even Lemur – and I'm not scared of changing. Because there will always *always* be the bins, and the den, and Cathkin, and Wibfipper, and the water fight, and a million other things we've done together. Nobody can ever take that from us. Because that's ours, for all time.